Recreate the elegant world of the Wild Rose Inn with this beautiful stencil. . . . Use it to decorate stationery, furniture, your bedroom, or any place you want to add a touch of timeless grace.

D1019814

"Fare thee well," Bridie said to the others still standing on the *Rose*. "God speed you."

Then she dropped her bundle over the side into the boat, and scrambled down the rope ladder. The new Marbleheaders found room among the cargoes and the rowers, and then the little boat made for the landing.

Bridie sat staring at her family on the dock. They looked uncertainly back at her, as though not daring to hope she was their daughter. Gusts of wind teased a few curls around Mistress MacKenzie's head, and the small boy at her side danced impatiently from foot to foot. Bridie met his eyes across the narrowing space of water between them, and a wide, thankful smile spread across her lips and was answered by him.

" 'Tis her, 'tis Bridget!" he piped up, tugging at his mother's sleeve.

"They are your family indeed," Mistress Carter said with a smile.

Bridie's vision swam as her eyes filled with tears again. She could barely see her father, tall and gaunt, as he stepped closer to the edge of the dock. The rowers bent their backs to the task, pulling the boat nearer and nearer. And then Bridie's mother held out her hand.

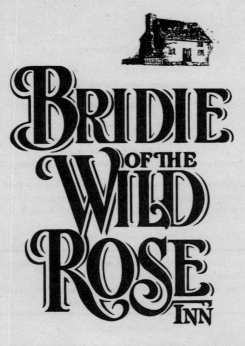

BRIDIE OF THE WILD ROSE INN

Jennifer Armstrong

BANTAM BOOKS

New York • *Toronto* • *London* • *Sydney* • *Auckland*

RL 5.0, 012 and up

BRIDIE OF THE WILD ROSE INN

A Bantam Book/February 1994

Wild Rose Inn™ is a trademark of Daniel Weiss Associates, Inc.

ISBN 0-553-29866-6

Published simultaneously in the United States and Canada

Bantam Books are published by Bantam Books, a division of Bantam Doubleday Dell Publishing Group, Inc. Its trademark, consisting of the words "Bantam Books" and the portrayal of a rooster, is Registered in U.S. Patent and Trademark Office and in other countries. Marca Registrada. Bantam Books, 1540 Broadway, New York, New York 10036.

PRINTED IN THE UNITED STATES OF AMERICA

OPM   0 9 8 7 6 5 4 3 2 1

BRIDIE
OF THE
WILD
ROSE
INN

Chapter One

BRIDIE MACKENZIE STOOD clutching her worn black cloak around her, the sharp wind pressing it to her back and keening in her ears.

"How can I leave?" she whispered.

"You can," her friend Kit replied. "You've spoken of nothing else these ten years since your mother and father went to Massachusetts Colony."

Bridie's heart leaped at the name of the place that was so far away from her beloved Scotland. Wherever she looked was the familiar and the known—the short street of Arrochar with its tiny stone houses, the slope of dour Ben Lomond rising behind them. For sixteen years it had been the whole range of her world. And now she was leaving for Glasgow with the Carter family, from there would go to Liverpool, and thence strike out across the great Atlantic.

"And I go into the wilderness," she said in amaze-

1

ment. She turned and gripped Kit's hand, her eyes shining. " 'Tis wonderful and strange, is it not?"

Kit shivered, for it was early March and the winter's ice was still unmelted on the high mountains. A tear shone at the corner of her eye, and Bridie felt all at once her home rushing from her like the roaring wind. She threw her arms around her friend and held tight to her. "I shall miss you dearly. How I wish you would come too."

"Nay, nay." Kit pulled away. "You're the brave bold one, not me. I could not make such a voyage."

"I'm not brave, nor bold," Bridie said, shaking her head and looking about her at the bleak, untenanted houses of Arrochar village. There was a bitterness in the air of old snow, mingled with the sweet smell of peat smoke, while high up somewhere an eagle screamed. Bridie's heart was filled with love and dismay. "I'm more frightened than I have been since Granddaddy died."

Behind them, a dray horse stamped on the flinty ground as the Carters finished loading the wagon. Their voices, and the voices of the folk seeing them off, were pitched low and cautious, for it was a great undertaking and all were awed by it. Bridie felt a pulling within her, and ducked her head so as not to see the home she was leaving.

"Here be the Father," Kit said in a hoarse voice.

Father Dougal, his weak blue eyes watering in the wind, came to the girls and made a cross over them. *"Nominy patry,"* he mumbled, his Latin as poor and forgotten as Scotland itself.

"Thank you, Father," Bridie whispered, tears rolling down her cheek.

"What's this? What would your grandfather say?"

Bridie sniffed. "He would say, 'Hearten yourself, my lass,'" she said with a smile that hurt her.

"And so hearten yourself, my lass," the priest told her with sad and simple love.

She lifted her chin. "I do. I will."

"Father, we are ready."

Master Carter stood behind them, his face set and afraid. He looked at Bridie and nodded, and the blood in her body raced with sudden alarm. She turned to Kit and clutched her hands. "Remember me."

Kit was crying and could not stop. "For always."

Now Bridie felt the earth spin under her. She could not credit what was happening to her, that she was truly leaving all she knew and loved behind her, and that she would travel the ocean and face unknown peril—this to join again the parents who had orphaned her. Her sight darkened, her breath caught in her throat, and she heard again her mother's voice. "Bridie. We mun tell you something hard."

At six, Bridie had not seen how poor and bare the life was, and only knew that her mother and father looked grave and fearful, and that it filled her with fear too. Her grandfather had sat hunched by the hearth, his hands hanging limp between his knees and his face stricken.

"What, Mama?" she asked.

Her father took her into his lap, and she felt him tremble. "We mun go away and leave you for some time," he said, and when she struggled her mother knelt before her and held her and cried.

"We love you, darling, but we must make a new home for you in another place."

Bridie did not hear that, had heard nothing after the first blow—her mother was leaving her, and her father as well. A sound started in her and rose, and came out as a wail. "Take me! Take me with you!"

" 'Tis too long a journey for a child," Master MacKenzie explained. "And we know not what awaits us."

"Granddaddy will be your father until we send for you," her mother said, kissing Bridie's hands. "And there's a Mother in heaven who will watch over you for me."

"Mama!"

"And look, darling," Mistress MacKenzie said, her voice breaking. She pulled something from her pocket and pressed a wooden doll into Bridie's lap. "A poppet. Look after it well for me and bring it with you when you come."

"You and I will go together," Granddaddy said.

Bridie looked from mother to father to the old man, then stared at the wooden poppet. She could not understand anything, for her world was flying into blackness.

"We will send for you, my little love," her mother promised, kissing again Bridie's cheeks and hair.

"Mama! Don't leave me!"

"We will send for you soon."

Soon.

But the days had drawn on, and Bridie had waited and dreamed of her parents for ten long years. Now her grandfather had died and she had to go on alone. She stood in the windy road, gripping the side of the wagon until her knuckles were white.

"Farewell, Granddaddy," she said, bowing her head.

Master Carter took her elbow. "Come, Mistress."

For a moment, she could not look up. But at last her sight cleared, and when she gazed behind her it was with her mother's eyes. She saw the poor town, and the people she loved and had to leave. Her heart ached, and she knew her mother had done this bitter thing for love.

She drew in her breath. "Let us go to Massachusetts, then. I've waited overlong already."

Bridie smiled at Father Dougal and Kit. "Farewell," she told them, and then climbed into the wagon.

Bridie awoke with a lurch in her dark corner, and held her balance as the ship pitched from side to side and from bow to stern. Then, as another wave hit the vessel across the beam, she cracked her head against the wooden planks of the cabin.

"Och, my head." She sighed, rubbing the sore spot with one hand. "I'll be cracked to pieces by the time this storm is done!"

The sloshing of water in the bilges was as loud as the water washing overhead on deck. The whole world above and below was water, loud and howling and cold, and only a few planks separated Bridie and the other passengers on the *Rose* from the black fathoms. She crossed herself in the dark as another wave smacked the ship broadside. From the other corners of the airless cabin, muffled voices, the cries of small children, and dispirited moans were the only sounds. The ship itself groaned like a live thing complaining against the battery of the storm. Bridie dragged herself upright and, braced against the bucking of the waves, felt her way to the spot the Carter family had claimed.

"I will go up to the deck," she whispered to them in the dark. "I cannot draw breath down here."

A feverish hand gripped hers. "We're nearly to port, aren't we?" Mistress Carter asked. "Nearly there?"

"I believe so," Bridie said quietly. "I pray so."

She freed her hand and made her way across the cramped space, clumsily striking her shins on a cradle and nearly upsetting the latrine bucket. Too much longer cooped up below would drive her mad. She clambered up the ladder, and then clawed anxiously at the hatchway before tumbling out from the shelter.

The wildness of the storm caught her breath and whipped her curling dark brown hair around her cheeks, then howled its curses into her ears. "Holy Saint Magnus!" she choked, turning her back to the stinging wind. She squinted against the rain. No landfall. No land. Only water.

A sailor thrust past her, yelling orders. Aloft, men clung like spiders in the rigging to take down sail. The masts and rails waved in broad, dizzying arcs above Bridie's head, and a ragged pennant cracked straight out, stiff in the wind, from the main shrouds. Bridie shrank back between two casks and tried to keep her heavy skirts

6

from being drenched as a wave swept across her feet. The deck was awash.

"Blessed Saint Mary, Saint Andrew, Saint Christopher!" she cried out to the storm. " 'Tis Bridget MacKenzie! I'm voyaging to Marblehead!"

In spite of her fear, she tipped her wet face to the sky. The rain was sweet and cold. The saints she had prayed to in Scotland could surely see her and protect her even across the ocean. But she would pray particularly loud to be heard across the distances and over the storm.

"Dinna forget me!" she added.

A hurrying figure passed her hiding place and then returned. The *Rose*'s mate peered between the casks at her and yanked her out.

"Get you below! This is no place for maids!"

Bridie wished she might object. After four weeks at sea, the cabin was a stinking prison to her. But then an arm of the gale threw her off her feet and pitched her toward the portside bulwark. The mate grabbed her and dragged her back toward the hatch.

"Get you below!" he roared.

Drenched, frozen, and trembling, Bridie fumbled the hatch open, watched a torrent of water cascade through, then fell below into the dark, cramped, and very wet cabin.

A round of complaints greeted her as she groped her way forward.

"This water!" a woman's voice scolded. "Our goods are all fairly drowned."

"Won't someone light the lantern?" called out a man feebly. "It's dark as doom."

Bridie hugged her arms around herself, knowing with a painful certainty that she had no dry clothes to put on. She was already wearing all she owned. Clenching her teeth to keep them from chattering, she made her way across the cabin, step by careful step, to her own berth near the Carters. She heard the unsteady tread of feet as someone went in search of a flame for the lantern. Something round was rolling back and forth across the cabin deck, hitting the bulwarks with dull wooden thumps.

"Is it always so cold in these parts?" Bridie asked, her breath coming in fits and starts as her shoulders quaked.

"I fear so," Mistress Carter replied. "I fear we're riding this storm right the way into Purgatory."

"Hush, woman," Master Carter said softly. "Remember the laws."

In the dark, Bridie's hand went to the tiny iron crucifix hanging at her throat under her dress. She pressed it protectively through the fabric, and as she did so, a faint, swaying light entered the cabin. Goodman Browning hung the lantern on a peg. The light shone dimly on the huddled collection of voyagers—Puritan and Catholic, fisherman and farmer, the tired wives, the sickly children.

"Is it true?" Bridie asked in an undertone. "About the laws? My parents wrote there are no priests."

"I have heard it is so," Master Carter said, dabbing at his scurvy-bleeding gums with the back of his hand. "They do say Massachusetts Colony admits none but the

Congregationals. No Quaker—no Catholic. We mun keep our devotions and our professions of faith private."

Mistress Carter stifled a moan. Her frightened face showed in and out of light and shadow as the lantern swung with the pitching ship. "We do go into Purgatory," she whispered. "We've had naught but sickness and foul skies on this ship, and the land we seek is filled with wolves and savages and Protestants."

"And the Protestants be the worst," Master Carter declared below his breath. "But it is Massachusetts where we must go to make our lives, for that is where the work is, laws or no."

Bridie cast a wary glance across the cabin at the other passengers. But none was paying them any mind, for all were too deeply sunk in their own miseries. Seasickness had plagued most of them throughout the voyage from Liverpool, and the rolling and bucking of the ship had sent even the halest and most stalwart to their narrow bunks. Some had been struck by the first stabs of scurvy, and nearly all were afflicted with the dysentery. Foul water, salt pork, wormy biscuit, and stale beer were in league against all the voyagers. The few who weren't ill tended those who were.

So, crowded and close as the quarters were, none had the strength or desire to eavesdrop on his fellows. Nevertheless, Bridie felt as uneasy as Master Carter did at his wife's loud lamentations over the Protestants. Catholics they were, all three, but they knew to keep it a closely guarded and burdensome secret. They did not even know if any of their fellow voyagers held the same faith. Generations of bloody division between Catholics and Presbyters had made religion a bitterly treasured thing to the Scots. Bridie knew the Protestants worshiped in their own way, but she had been raised in her Catholic faith, and it was inseparable from her.

Her eyes closed, and she saw again the tiny parish church in Arrochar, gray, lichen-scaled, with broken fragments of ancient stone crosses here and there among the grass tussocks, where she had so often bounded after hares in the twilight. And now, by straining, Bridie could almost hear the high, quavery voice of Father Dougal, telling her, at ten years old, how Saint Mary watched over her and her distant parents.

"Think of the Blessed Mother in heaven," he'd said, rubbing his arthritic knees with his blunt hands. "There she is, holding you in one hand and your mother and father in the other. And soon, she'll bring her hands together."

And with that, he had placed Bridie's palms together in a gesture of prayer, and Bridie's eyes had grown wide with hope.

It had given her comfort in those hard years, knowing the saints took such a particular care, and that Saint Mary watched her as her mother had promised. And she'd been sure that with so many of them to help her, she'd be joined with her parents again.

With her eyes still closed, she said a silent prayer of thanks. Then, behind the Carters, on the bunk nearest the bulwark, a fitful crying started up. Bridie opened her eyes as Mistress Carter turned and leaned across, murmuring quietly.

"How does little Margaret?" Bridie asked, kneeling beside the older woman. "Poor wee thing."

Margaret Carter, only seven years old, lay in a dry fever under a blanket. Her cheeks were sunk enough for the light to cast hollow shadows within them. As her mother laid a hand on her brow, the child whimpered.

"Can she still not keep anything in her stomach?" Bridie asked.

"Nay. Not a thing." Mistress Carter's face twitched with terrible emotion. "Not a thing. Nor does the fever break."

Master Carter looked on in dark, lost silence, and then pushed himself away. Bridie nodded. What little she knew of nursing and dosing she knew from the women of Arrochar, and from the grandfather who had taught her the names and properties of plants. Bridie had sat by many a sickbed and collected many a leaf and root in her years. Some of the herbs she knew were for uncommon complaints and rare afflictions, but Margaret's suffering was of an everyday nature.

Bridie searched her memory. There were countless herbal physics and simples for fever and distemper of the stomach, and the plants could be plucked from any grass-grown bank or in any garden plot. They couldn't be gathered on the heaving plains of the ocean, however. Bridie opened the bundle that held all her belongings, and groped blindly until her fingers touched a small, cloth-wrapped packet. She pulled it out and worked at the knotted laces.

"I have some small store of remedies," she whispered to Mistress Carter. "Yet these plants were gathered last summer and may have little potency left."

The woman bowed her head. "I can do nothing more. Help my Maggie."

"Master Carter," Bridie whispered, standing and drawing near the silent man. "Will you fetch a small dram of ale?"

He hurried away, steadying himself against the unruly motion of the ship. In her berth, Margaret made small, pained animal sounds. Bridie touched the girl's cheek.

"Don't fash yourself, my lassie," she crooned. "Hush, now."

When the child's father returned, Bridie took the wooden tumbler of beer and poured in the last remnants of dried and powdered wormwood from the packet. It would taste bitter and dry, and Bridie would have put in spearmint or crushed fennel seeds if she'd had them, or better still, honey mixed in withal. As it was, Margaret would have to choke it down in all its galling bitterness. Gently, tenderly, Bridie slipped her arm beneath the child's shoulders and raised her up. Margaret's eyes flickered open, but did not focus.

Bridie fed the girl in tiny sips, praying that Margaret was still too dazed and dreamy to notice the taste. She began a soft, murmuring monologue to keep her own spirits up while she dosed the little girl.

"Soon we'll be to Massachusetts," she whispered, repeating a litany she'd said many times on board. "And I'll see my own mother and father once more. I'll see my brother, John, whom I've not ever met, for he was born seven years ago in Marblehead. He's sure to be a fine, strong child, just as you are. I know you will be well very soon and will see your father making such fine boats as this one."

Humming softly under her breath, Bridie swirled the dregs of the ale around in the tumbler, and then tipped it into Margaret's mouth. The child made a weak attempt to spit it out, but Bridie bade her hush again. As Mistress Carter bent down to take Margaret into her arms, Bridie slipped out of the berth and went to her own hard and narrow bunk. She lay down, pulling an old cloak around herself.

Lying still, breathing quietly, Bridie tried to forget the ache in her bones by looking out at the crowded, stuffy, ill-lit cabin. All the people she saw were going to what they deemed new lives, new work, new chances in a new land. They had pried themselves from village and farm, limited their stocks and stores to mere handfuls, and stepped bravely out onto the salt waves. Bridie's parents had made the journey ten years earlier. Now she was finally following the light they had lit to lead her to them from Arrochar under Ben Lomond, to Glasgow and Liverpool and so onto the *Rose*.

Of what had happened with her family since they left Scotland, she knew very little. Once or maybe twice in a year, a short letter was carried to her grandfather by someone who had journeyed east. Father Dougal, himself barely literate, had carefully pieced out the words in those letters until Bridie had gotten them all to heart. Yet they told her painfully little: they spoke sketchily of a tavern, what the New Englanders called an ordinary; of her brother; of the hardships of settling into a new country. From those few words over the last ten years Bridie had conjured brilliant pictures in her mind, and she had always placed herself in those warm, sun-washed scenes.

Her fingers again went to her throat and touched the cross hidden beneath her dress. In her memory she could scarcely recall her mother's face, nor her father's, nor could she dream up an image of her brother, John. But it mattered very little. Bridie would see them for herself, God willing, very soon. No pain, no fear, no trial by fire was too dear a price for that. She closed her eyes and began to pray, and not long after fell asleep.

Chapter Two

By MORNING, the storm had abated. Bridie lay still for a moment when she awoke, relishing the gentle rocking of the ship. All the untoward, violent movement from the storm was over and done with. The daily matins of coughing, yawning, sniffling, and moaning filled the cabin with dreary sound. With one quick motion, Bridie rolled out of her berth, drew her cloak around her, and readied to go up on deck.

But before she left the cabin, she stopped to see how Margaret fared. Mistress Carter, red-eyed and drawn, sat by the child's side.

"How does she?" Bridie whispered.

"You can see," Mistress Carter said, pulling aside the child's covers.

Bridie's heart warmed at the sight of the sweat on Margaret's brow. The mother pressed a cloth to her daughter's face, and then drew up the covers again.

"She'll be improving by leaps and bounds now," Bridie said, smiling.

"Saint Mary knows what you've done." Mistress Carter looked up at Bridie and nodded her weary gratitude. "I never had the hand for using medicine as you've shown. I thank God you're here."

"Master Carter? Where is he?" Bridie asked.

"On the deck. We're near to port, they say."

Startled, Bridie ran to the ladder and climbed up, twisting her heavy hair into a knot at the back of her head as she went. The moment she lifted away the hatch, she was assailed by brilliant sunlight. It drew a laugh from her.

"Good morrow, Mistress MacKenzie," Master Carter said as she joined him at the rail. "Fine weather at last."

"We've Saint Christopher to thank for that," Bridie said, pushing aside a stray curl that the breeze kept playing with. The ship plied steadily within sight of land, plowing through the waves with bounding, spray-throwing speed. Bridie leaned forward as though she could urge the ship on even faster with her own desire.

"What country is that?" she asked, breathing deeply.

"Massachusetts," Master Carter said. "It looks fair."

"Fair indeed!" Bridie exclaimed. "I'll kiss each rock and tree when we're landed. I'm so tired with this voyage, to be sure I'd jump out here and now—if only I knew how to swim!"

"We'll make harbor soon enough," the man said.

"Not soon enough for me," she went on, impatient as ever. "Give us a westlin' wind to blow us home."

"You have no fears at all, do you?"

Bridie laughed and shook her head, though her heart fluttered. She had fears aplenty, but she refused to carry them with her to shore.

For several minutes they stood there looking at the place that would be their new continent. It was scarcely anything but a dark smudge beyond the brilliant water, but it rested there somberly, like the edge of something vast and magnificent and frightening.

With a shiver, Bridie scanned the waters to port and starboard. She spotted fishing vessels on each side, the small, squat boats with full-bellied sails that haunted the great fishing banks offshore. The waters of Massachusetts were said to teem with life. Tales had reached Scotland of the fat-clawed lobster, clams to dig up by the barrowful, eels, mussels, and all manner of fish—hake, haddock, and herring, the alewife, the flounder, and the turbot.

And most vital of all was the giant cod fairly leaping into the holds until the tiny boats wallowed under the rich, scaly load. It was cod that fed and peopled Marblehead, cod that drew the fisherfolk of Scotland and Cornwall to settle the rugged coasts and swell the ranks of the boatmakers and sailmakers, merchants and seamen, and cod that brought the gold of Europe to fatten Massachusetts's coffers. Bridie wished she could see one of the legendary fish. She was sure she'd taste it very soon.

Overhead, strident gulls let out their keening shrieks as they raced the ship, and the small, streamlined terns plummeted like hurled stones into the waves to pluck out silver-glinting fish. Surrounding all was the brilliant light,

17

reflected forever between the ocean and sky, filling the sails until they shone, cresting the ship's wake, and hanging luminously over the land like a divine aura. Bridie hugged her arms about herself. "Oh, when will we see Marblehead?" she asked.

Master Carter spotted the *Rose*'s captain by the binnacle and went to speak with him. Bridie watched from her post at the rail, squinting in the fresh light and feeling her heart race with excitement. Soon she'd be with her family in Massachusetts, and the old scrimping, scraping days in poor, barren Scotland would be behind her.

"Yon's Swampscott," Master Carter told her when he returned. He nodded toward the distant shore. "Marblehead is very near."

Bridie turned eagerly. At that distance, all she could make of the town of Swampscott was drifting smoke and clear pasturage breaking up the woods behind.

"It must be a sorry, tiny place," Bridie said. "Won't Marblehead be larger?"

"I don't know. We'll soon see."

"In my mind I can see it already," Bridie said. "With tall houses and broad streets, and the harbor filled with gallant ships. My family's ordinary is on Front Street. 'Tis sure to be a fine establishment, with the folk tipping their hats to my mother and father, and the gentry of the town taking their ease by our fire."

Master Carter cast a skeptical glance back Swampscott way, but said nothing. His thoughts no doubt were full of his own family's prospects and of the life he hoped to make for them by building boats. Bridie leaned forward

18

as the *Rose* coasted around a low lump of land. A small, stony island, spiked with pines and browsed by scruffy sheep, slipped by to starboard.

Then a long, narrow, rock-rimmed harbor opened up to port, with a gathering of tiny gray houses huddled around the edge like a collection of ragged seabirds' nests. Beyond was a knobby hill crowned with a plain, drab building. Here was another of the grim Puritan outposts, Bridie presumed. The mate yelled orders to the crew, and sailors leaped up into the rigging.

"What can be this other place?" Bridie asked, making a fist in her impatience. "When will we be at Marblehead?"

The mate arched his brows. "Momently," he said.

"Och, no!" Bridie gasped, looking more intently at the small, colorless settlement before them. "Can it be?"

"Aye," the mate replied. "Yon's the Marble Harbor. This be your new home."

Chapter Three

BRIDIE'S THROAT CLOSED with sudden tears, and she shook her head in confusion.

"Hearten yourself, Mistress MacKenzie," Master Carter warned. "There is no turning back."

"But—" Bridie put one hand to her flyaway curls, as though her very thoughts were being scattered by the wind. There were no fine broad streets or tall houses here. There was only a higgledy-piggledy maze of crooked ways climbing around the rocks, small bits of houses tucked into the cracks, and row upon row of wooden racks along the water's edge, above which circled great companies of screaming, fighting seabirds. The light seemed no longer golden but harsh and glaring. Bridie's eyes stung with salt spray and tears.

"Fish flakes," Master Carter said, nodding at the racks. "They say 'tis where they do dry the cod."

Bridie looked on with dismay. Because she could not reconcile the drab, dreary harbor town ahead of her with the image in her mind, the rolling of the deck beneath her feet accorded well with the unsteadiness of her heart. She was all asea.

"I thought it would be otherwise," she said in a low voice as the ship nosed into the harbor.

Fishing boats bobbed at anchor near the cluster of waterside buildings, their bows all pointed stubbornly into the inrushing tide. Near the flakes a gang of boys tossed rocks and shells when the birds dared too close to the precious fish. Each time a lad let fly, the flocks scattered raucously into the air. Then, as the ship drew nearer, a pair of boys broke away from the gang and ran up to the town, dodging the flakes and hurdling the unwieldy boulders that lay about.

From up in the town, Bridie heard a low bass note sound on a conch-shell horn. The tone rippled out to meet the ship in wave after wave of sound through the bright air, vibrating in Bridie's rib cage and raising the hair on her arms and the back of her neck. The note sounded again and again, almost unearthly, like the voice of the ocean itself. Bridie felt her heart lift.

"It is a wee scrap of a place, to be sure," she said, breathing unsteadily. "But they must be hardy souls to cling to such a spot."

"Aye, and to thrive here," Master Carter agreed.

All about them, the ship's crew was in a welter of activity, taking in sails, readying the lines, and calling out the channel markings. The passengers, blink eyed and pale, climbed on deck and stood at the rails to gape at Marblehead. The weeks at sea had been a known hardship. But now new and unknown challenges were to start in earnest. They had arrived.

Nearer and nearer the ship plied, and Bridie leaned forward again. Now she could see people in the town coming down to the wooden dock. A sudden fit of shyness swept a blush across her face. She had no confidence that the people of Marblehead would welcome her, a girl with no skills but a few simple cures. That was little enough to bring to a place such as Marblehead, wedged as it was between a vast ocean in front and a vast wilderness behind. Surely the folk here looked for fellows strong enough to help hold back the tides and the forest.

And would her own parents hold their arms out to her? She had sent word that her grandfather had died, and they had sent for her, asking Father Dougal to help secure her passage and to seek traveling companions. But that letter had been as thrifty of news as all the others. They'd said "Come to Massachusetts now," and she was coming. Bridie closed her eyes and pressed her shaking fingers against her throat, feeling for the cross. They had always meant to send for her, but it had been so long. . . .

Blessed Saint Mary, she prayed. *You've looked after me this far. Keep your eye on me a little longer. See me into my parents' house, and I'll find my way from there.*

The shouts of the seamen made her open her eyes, and as she did so, she spied a trio on the dock—man, woman, and small boy. A shock traveled from her heart clear down to her chilled feet and left her pulse in a tumult.

"Jesu," she whispered. "There they are."

Her heart pounding, Bridie craned forward to make them out. The saved-up memories of ten years ago came back to her as she tried to make out the faces of the man and the woman. They were her parents: Ian and Flora MacKenzie. Tears welled up in her eyes and spilled out, but she could not lift her hand to wave. She was too frightened.

"Is this truly it?" Mistress Carter said, appearing suddenly at Bridie's elbow with Margaret bundled against her shoulder. Her forehead was creased as she gazed at Marblehead.

"Aye," Bridie whispered, straining to see. "We debark here."

Her heart jolted suddenly at the thought of her belongings still below deck. For one moment, she wished she might simply leave it all behind. If she was to start anew, why not start with empty hands?

But then she thought of the few treasures she had so carefully preserved. She turned and flew down to the cabin.

"Don't let them forget to let me off," she whispered to any saint who might be listening. "I've done with this ship!"

With a mad scramble, she gathered her few meager things into a bundle in her cloak and tied it all with a thin leather strap. As she stood to leave, she cast one last look around at the low-ceilinged, foul-smelling room that had been her home for weeks. Already it had a deserted air. There were a few worthless things scattered about: a cracked clay cup lay discarded in one corner, beside a bunk was a broken knife, and just at her feet Bridie saw a bent nail. Without thinking, she picked it up and slipped it into her pocket. Iron could always be reused, and it was against her nature to let a scrap go to waste.

Then, taking one last look at the stuffy place, Bridie ran out and climbed up to the deck again, her bundle bumping against her knee.

Sailors brushed past her, voyagers milled on deck for a view of the new world, and the mate shouted orders to let down a boat as the ship lay still in the harbor.

"Get you into the boat," Master Carter advised. His wife and child were already aboard, settling themselves amid their baggage. Mistress Carter shielded Margaret from the cool breeze with her cloak.

"Fare thee well," Bridie said to the others still standing on the *Rose*. "God speed you."

Then she dropped her bundle over the side into the boat, and scrambled down the rope ladder. The new Marbleheaders found room among the cargoes and the rowers, and then the little boat made for the landing.

Bridie sat staring at her family on the dock. They looked uncertainly back at her, as though not daring to hope she was their daughter. Gusts of wind teased a few curls around Mistress MacKenzie's head, and the small boy at her side danced impatiently from foot to foot. Bridie met his gaze across the narrowing space of water between them, and looked into eyes just like her own. A wide, thankful smile spread across her lips and was answered by him.

"'Tis her, 'tis Bridget!" he piped up, tugging at his mother's sleeve.

"They are your family indeed," Mistress Carter said with a smile.

Bridie's vision swam as her eyes filled with tears again. She could barely see her father, tall and gaunt, as he stepped closer to the edge of the dock. The rowers bent their backs to the task, pulling the boat nearer and nearer. And then Bridie's mother held out her hand.

"Mother!" Bridie called, her voice choked. The last ten years flew backward in a blink, and Bridie was six again, running to her mother's strong, enfolding arms.

The moment the boat bumped against the dock, Bridie jumped up, setting the craft rocking.

"Take heed!" a sailor charged as the boat tipped wildly and shipped water.

Bridie only saw her mother and father and brother reaching out to bring her home. Arms grabbed hers, and she began to cry with relief the moment her feet hit the rough wooden dock. "Mother!" she sobbed.

"Bridie, lass, you're here," Mistress MacKenzie said, holding her so close that Bridie could scarcely breathe. "We've waited too long for this day!"

Bridie pressed her face hard against her mother's shoulder, taking in a wild mix of impressions all at once: that she was as tall as her mother now, that Mistress Mac-Kenzie still smelled the same and sounded the same, and that the arms that held her close felt thin and bony, and trembled under the weight of emotion.

"My darling girl," her mother whispered.

Bridie laughed and tried to check her crying, though her heart was racing with joy and relief. "I thought I'd never last the voyage out."

" 'Twas rough and wearying when we did it, I remember well. But you look fresh as a robin," Mistress MacKenzie said, taking Bridie's face in both her hands. The lines of care around her eyes folded as she smiled, and made creases that caught her tears. "What a fine, bonny girl you are. As I knew you would be."

Bridie laughed again and gave her father a swift hug, but her heart wrenched as she saw how much he looked like her beloved grandfather. She knew her granddaddy was watching from heaven and smiling though, so she did not feel too sad. Her mother pulled her close again with a sob, and Bridie closed her eyes with relief. She was home.

Then she turned to look at the small boy standing shyly behind their mother. He peeped out at her.

"And who might be this proper boy?" she asked, charmed by his smile.

"My name is John MacKenzie."

"Good speed an' further to you, Johnny," Bridie sang. "Good health, hale hands, and weather bonny."

Brother and sister grinned at one another delightedly for a moment. Then, for no reason, both laughed, and a gull hovering overhead laughed too.

"I'll rule the roost now that I'm here," Bridget warned John with a smile. "Take heed not to cross me, for I warn you, I'm a proper screaming skelpie-limmor when I'm angered."

"Don't believe her, Johnny," Master MacKenzie said.

"She was always a laughing, dancing fairy of a child." He smiled at her again, and then the lines around his mouth deepened. "How did my father die? Well and peaceful?"

Bridie's memory flew back to Arrochar, to the kind, rough-handed man who had raised her, been her mother and father and friend since she was six years old. She had nursed him through his illness and closed his eyes at the last. She bowed her head for a moment in respect of his memory and then raised her eyes to her father's face.

"He died well and peaceful," she said softly.

"Thank God for that." Master MacKenzie shook his head. "And the folk around and nearby looked after you well when he was gone?"

"Yes, Father." Bridie squeezed his hand. She sensed, without being told, that her parents felt a heavy weight for leaving her behind for ten long years. But now they were united again, and Bridie felt nothing but hope and joy.

Around them on the dock, folk were unloading the crates and barrels of wares from the ship, and the Carters stood by, overseeing the removal of their things. Bridie noticed several pairs of eyes trained her way, curious, no doubt, about the newcomer and the bright, loud happiness surrounding the MacKenzies. There were men and women, grayly dressed in wool, with leather gauntlets, wooden pattens, and felt hats.

Her father cleared his throat gruffly and lifted her bundle. "Let us get from here, where we're in the way."

Bridie grabbed her little brother's hand.

"Take me home," she said.

With her face tilted toward the April sun, Bridie

strode beside her brother, stepping off the dock into the muddy dockyard. A pig wallowed noisily beside a pile of offal, squealing and grunting with bliss. The storm had left the dirt streets mired so that there was hardly a dry step to be taken. People slogged through the grime and mud, nodding to the MacKenzies as they passed.

"I never thought Massachusetts would be so wet," Bridie said, picking her way around a puddle. The wooden heels of her shoes were heavily clumped with mud, and a bedraggled chicken made a noisy, flustering dash across their path. "This is a—"

With a shriek, Bridie toppled over backward as her foot slid out from under her. She landed with a soft splash in a puddle. After the first shock of landing, she began to laugh.

"You were always a clumsy one," Bridie's mother said.

"The fairies get under my feet to trip me," Bridie explained. Her eyes gleamed as she looked up from the mud.

John held his hand out to her, and then crouched at her side. "What is this?"

He put one finger to Bridie's throat. She looked down to see her crucifix dangling free on its chain.

Her parents looked down also, and Mistress MacKenzie's face tightened. "You'd best take that off and leave it off," she said, darting a quick glance up the narrow street. Some people had stopped to look at Bridie still sitting in the puddle.

"What is it?" John repeated, his eyes wide. "Is it a charm like the Indian sagamores wear?"

"Och, no," Bridie said. She struggled to her feet in the mud, and covered the crucifix with one protective hand. "There's nothing heathen about it. It's the cross our Lord was—"

"Bridget!"

She stopped. Her father's face was grim, and the lines from his nose down to the corners of his mouth were set and deep.

"We're in the Congregation now," he said in a quiet voice. "They hold with no idols—"

Bridie felt her face flush hot and scarlet. She'd known her parents could not be practicing Catholics anymore, and known that they were attending the Puritan meeting. But she had assumed that was only for show, to conform to local custom. To her ears now it sounded as though they'd truly broken with their faith. "This is no idol, as well you know," she whispered.

Mistress MacKenzie tucked the crucifix back into Bridie's chemise. "Take it off and leave it off nonetheless," she repeated, looking intently into Bridie's eyes. "Please, daughter. For us. I wouldn't want anyone to think ill of you."

Bridie met her mother's gaze, feeling a strange wrench within her breast. "But, Mother. God—"

"God has His own designs in Massachusetts," Mistress MacKenzie said, her voice low and urgent. "And you're not to question them."

Bridie looked down at her brother, at her parents, at

the crooked, muddy streets with their huddling houses, and at the glittering harbor beyond. It was all different from Scotland. All different.

"I will put it away," Bridie said. "But I cannot put away my faith."

"Be that as it may," replied her father gently. "But you'll come to meeting with us on Sabbath. It's the law. Take a careful advisement from me."

Bridie bowed her head. Her jaw ached from the clenching of her teeth. "I will."

"Now, let us get home," Mistress MacKenzie said more gently. "We needn't stand in the mud all the day long."

Bridie smiled, putting her weary concerns behind her. "Yes. I'm all aflitter to see where we live."

"We have the ordinary on Front Street," John told her proudly. "And we have a full house on Sabbath and other days too."

"And you brew the best ale in Massachusetts, do you?" Bridie asked him.

As they made their way up Front Street, Bridie noticed several passersby looking at her with open curiosity. A pair of young men with muskets across their shoulders smiled shyly at her as they passed. Bridie ducked her head and put on a modest expression. On all sides were signs of the fish that gave life to the town: nets strung between houses for repair, lobster pots stacked by the doorsills, oars propped against fences, and in every sunny spot, fish flakes with their burden of gutted cod. The salt smell was everywhere, like the mewing of the gulls and the light

30

glaring off the water. There was a freshness to everything that Bridie liked. A woman with rolled-up sleeves and raw red arms opened a door and tossed a bucketful of fish heads into the street, and the dogs and gulls made a mad dash for it.

"Here we are," Master MacKenzie said, stopping before a small gray dwelling that stood hard by the street.

Bridie stepped back for a full view. What reared up in front of her was a square story-and-a-half house cased in weathered clapboard. Two small leaded-glass windows on the ground floor opened onto the town. Above, an even tinier square window looked out at the harbor. The roof was shingled with wood, and there were touches of red paint at the windows and door. A stone chimney climbed up one end, spouting smoke. To the side of the building was a yard fenced with posts and withies to keep the roving pigs from ransacking the vegetable patch.

"Welcome," said Mistress MacKenzie.

Bridie's heart flooded with warmth. She was home.

"Come in," John pleaded, pulling hard on her hand.

Bridie smiled at him and turned to view her new town once more before she went in. Walking down the street was a handsome young man in sober attire, with a sour-faced older woman at his side. He paused, and met Bridie's gaze full on. Bridie nodded a greeting. She judged him her own age or just older.

"Stop gawking," the woman scolded, yanking him by the arm.

He flushed and hurried on.

"Who were they?" Bridie asked her mother as she stepped onto the threshhold. "That was a queer woman."

"Goodwife Handy and her lad, Will of God Handy," Mistress MacKenzie said. "Just come from Salem, they are. Her husband was lost at sea sometime since, and now she has taken a license for another ordinary."

"And a dour, dark, overpious woman she is," Master MacKenzie added. "Such as all that lot in Salem are. They see witches in their daily bread."

"Witches?" Bridie began to cross herself, but then awkwardly dropped her hand to her side. "Are there witches here?"

Her father shouldered her tight-wrapped bundle and shook his head. "We've no time to go looking for witches in Marblehead. There's fishing to be done. Now, come you in, lassie."

There was no space at all between house and street, and Bridie saw she would get from one to the other in a single step. She closed her eyes and sprang across the doorstep into the house. Then she looked.

She was in the center of a low-ceilinged room, the rough-hewn beams darkened by smoke, and a broad, deep fireplace with a roaring fire at one end.

"A wood fire!" Bridie gasped, amazed by the extravagance. "Nay, you shouldn't have done it for me. That's such a muckle of wood!"

"But what else should we burn?" John asked in astonishment.

Mistress MacKenzie swung the iron crane out of the fire and lifted the lid of a pot that hung from it. "In Scotland we burned peat and turves, for there was scarcely any wood at all. But here the forest goes on forever, Bridie. We might burn wood day and night for an eternity and never see the end of it."

Bridie stared wonderingly at the dancing fire and at the objects that glinted in its light. A long plank table occupied the center of the room, flanked by scarred wooden benches. A large press stood against one wall, its shelves lined with wooden and leathern tankards, and two of pewter. Crockery and wooden dishes were there also, and porringers and bowls. Iron-bound chests lined the walls, and tallow candles hung in bunches from the ceiling.

"It's very fine," Bridie said, glowing with happiness. "Very fine." She stepped backward to take it all in and tipped over a bench with a clatter. John giggled as he put it right.

"I'm clumsy as any cow," Bridie said to him behind her hand, and he laughed merrily again. "I might knock the whole house tapsalteerie if I'm not careful."

"Come," Mistress MacKenzie said. "Sit you down and tell us all the news while we eat. We've much to learn about each other."

"Sit by me." John wriggled with excitement on the bench and turned shining eyes to his newfound sister. "Sit by me, Bridie."

She bent down to fold him in a quick hug. "I love you already, you bonny bairn. I'll sit by you and gladly."

Soon the scarred plank table was filled with wooden trenchers of dusty bread baked in the ashes, tankards of beer, and a pot of fish stew. Each in turn speared chunks of fish with a knife and set them on slabs of bread.

"I've been longing for real food these many weeks," Bridie said, relishing the yeasty smell as she tore a crust. "Biscuit and salt pork make a drab dinner."

"We have all manner of game and good foods here," her father told her, catching a drip of fish broth on his chin with the back of his hand. "Venison and turkey and moose-deer—"

"And rabbits and partridge—" John put in.

"Dewberry, blueberry, pompion, squash, maize, nuts of all kind—" their mother said.

They were laughing, vying to list the most good things to eat, and Bridie looked from one to another with growing astonishment. In Scotland, where much of the diet was oats, and where most game was the property of the landowners, such bounty was reserved for lords and princes.

"The food is all here for the taking," Master MacKenzie said. "This is indeed a land of plenty."

" 'Tis why so many people come," Mistress MacKenzie explained.

"There is a cost, however," Bridie's father said thoughtfully, soaking up the rich broth with a chunk of bread. "The cost is conformity."

Bridie felt the smile fade from her lips. She heard the warning in her father's voice and also the regret, and a shadow of uneasiness crept into her heart. "I do hear you," she said with quiet emphasis. "But you must know Father Dougal has been my family with Granddaddy."

"We know," Mistress MacKenzie replied, exchanging a look with her husband. "We know it full well."

John sat, unaware of the sober words, counting off kinds of berries on his fingers.

"Strawberries too!" he piped up into the silence.

Bridie laughed in spite of herself. "Strawberries? I'm very greedy for those and will find it hard to save you any if I find some."

"You will?" John asked, crestfallen.

She grinned. "Nay, I'm only playing with you. You shall have the first strawberries I find, I promise you."

While Bridie finished her food, her parents asked questions of the old friends back home, and she told them all she could. Her parents both looked melancholy as they harked back to their days in Scotland, but Mistress Mac-Kenzie was the first to put away her wistful sighs.

"Folk will be by soon," she said as she stood to begin clearing the meal. "They'll all want to see the new Mac-Kenzie."

"And I'll want to see all of them, as well," Bridie said eagerly.

Her father rose from the table. "Johnny and I can show you the rest of the place."

Bridie took her brother's hand and swung it from side to side. "Convey me to my apartments, good sir," she said as he giggled.

Master MacKenzie opened a door opposite the one they'd entered, and led the way into another keeping room. A wooden bedstead was tucked under a steep ladder to the floor above. John scrambled up this ladder, beckoning Bridie on.

"We've another real bed up here," he said with pride. "We've got it new for you and me to share."

Bridie could scarcely take in all she saw. The ordinary was sparely furnished, with nothing fancy to soften the lines. But every space was crammed with stores of some kind: chests of clothing and boxes of rare spices, linens, and tanned hides. As she climbed the ladder behind her brother, she saw even more stores packed above. In the forward room, the room with the window, a bed was indeed wedged in between barrels of flour and kegs of spirit. A bunch of onions hung from a nail, and coils of hempen rope filled one corner.

"I'll feel like a queen among such plenty," Bridie said, sitting on the bed beside John.

"You mun unpack your things," her father said, setting down her bundle on the small scrap of open floor space. "Now that we're back, we'll be getting custom downstairs."

Already Bridie heard the door opening and shutting down below, and voices filling the tavern. She hurried to untie the laces.

"What did you bring from Scotland?" John asked, his eyes alive with curiosity.

"Very little," Bridie told him. "I sold what I had for passage, and forbye I was told not to bring much on the ship."

As she spoke, her nimble fingers unknotted the

leather straps, and she unfolded the unwieldy bundle on the bed. One of her few precious treasures tumbled out.

"What is it?" John asked, picking up the small mirror.

"My keekin' glass," Bridie said. "Did you never see yourself before? You're a rare handsome fellow, you know."

John held the mirror up to his face and turned this way and that, grinning and making faces at himself. His square, elfin face was as brown as a nut from the sun, and his short-cropped hair tawny also. "And what else have you?"

Bridie tenderly unwrapped a cotton kerchief from around her wooden doll. Her voice caught in her throat as she whispered, "This was my poppet from when I was a tiny child no bigger than a chicken. I couldn't leave it behind me, could I?"

John showed little interest in the crude wooden doll. He placed it beside the mirror and picked up one last carefully wrapped bundle.

"And what is this?" he asked.

Bridie hugged it to her heart. "Most precious of all."

"Golden coins, is it?"

"Nay," Bridie laughed. "Look here."

After taking off the laces, she removed the oiled marten skin, took away the damp fleece, and showed John three black sticks. His face fell.

"What are they?"

"Roses," Bridie whispered. "From our grandfather's house."

"We have roses here," John told her in a puzzled voice. "They grow on the sea cliffs."

Bridie nodded, but her thoughts were filled with a picture of her grandfather taking a moment of ease in the late day, tenderly coaxing his rosebush into bloom. "It may be I can plant one here and graft these slips onto it. 'Tis a lovely, bonny red rose."

"You need not have brought one all the way from Scotland," her brother chided.

"So say you!" Bridie snapped her fingers at him and stood up to find room for her things in the crowded garret.

Laughter drifted up from downstairs with the sound of booted feet. The MacKenzie ordinary was back in trade. John slipped out of the room, calling Bridie to follow him.

For a moment, she paused. She still reeled from the newness of everything, from meeting her family again and seeing her home. To face a crowd of strangers was something she didn't yet have the courage for.

As the rumble of voices continued, Bridie knelt down on the floor and shoved aside a box. Through an ample gap between the floorboards, she could see into the tavern room below. She bent down to listen.

"Your daughter voyaged safe from Scotland, we hear," said one man. "Be she a Catholic as you once were?"

Mistress MacKenzie stooped over to place a tankard on the table. "Nay, nay. Bridget is a good Protestant now."

Bridie sat up abruptly, her face burning, and from habit her fingers went to the cross at her throat. She whispered a prayer to Saint Mary, shaking her head with the pain of her mother's words. Her mother herself had given Bridie at birth into Saint Mary's care, but now would not own her. It wounded her so that she covered her eyes and could not breathe for a moment.

She rose and went to the window. Through it, she saw the gleaming ocean and the all-encompassing brilliant light. It was as though she were still on board the *Rose* and had not yet reached safe harbor. But harbor she would find. Of that she was determined. Bridie pulled the chain from around her neck and put the cross away.

Chapter Four

BRIDIE WAS AWAKENED on her first full day in Marblehead when a shaft of sunlight laid itself like a warm hand across her cheek. She stirred in the bed, suddenly aware of another body beside hers, and heard the faint, rustling whisper of straw beneath her.

"Good morrow to you, Johnny," she said, pushing off the cover and touching his forehead with one finger. "A fine Sunday it is."

John rolled over, hitching the blanket higher over his shoulder.

Pulling her cloak around her, Bridie crossed the small, cramped chamber to the window. She had to shield her eyes to look out, as the early-spring sun shone straight in through the diamond-shaped panes. She could see nothing through the glare. But beyond, somewhere nearby, was the meeting house. She knew she was expected to attend the Sabbath day service, like it or no.

With a sigh, she turned away. She would make the

best of it. God and the saints would know where her heart and her faith truly were. She put a smile on her face and then ripped the covers from her sleepy brother. "On your feet, my Johnny!" she sang out.

Not long after, the MacKenzies left the ordinary in a group and joined the line of worshipers trailing up Front Street. The morning air held a tight spring chill, and Bridie felt the salt breeze rolling off the water and wrapping itself around her neck. She shivered and ducked her head.

Then, as they turned up a beaten pathway that led up a rise, Bridie lifted her gaze and saw a grinning, bloody wolf's head before her, nailed to the wall of the meeting house with an iron spike. She drew in her breath sharply.

"Jesu," she exclaimed. She crossed herself by instinct, heedless of her parents' worried frowns. "What devilry is this?"

Her father squinted at the bloody thing. "The town pays fifteen shillings for any wolf's head to the man who brings it in," he said. "The wolves savage the flocks, and even do sometimes kill a child."

Bridie stood rooted to the pathway, her heart tripping and stumbling as she stared at the grisly thing. Blood had dripped down the rough planking of the meeting house, and a fly buzzed hungrily among the coarse and matted fur of the neck. She noticed similar red-brown stains at intervals along the side of the building. She could only guess at the number of such prizes the meeting house had sported over time.

Bridie felt the hair on her arms stand up as she

looked around at the people of the congregation who passed her. Men with muskets, children with large dogs, women with hard and careworn faces. What kind of savagery did they live in? Who were they to put such gruesome adornments on their house of God? Then she noticed three men on the outskirts of the crowd, men with red-gold skin and outlandish attire—Indians. Bridie's eyes widened in fright, but no one else seemed to mind their presence. Perhaps they were not of the savage tribes, she thought, looking wildly around. The three Indians only stood and watched the Sabbath procession and made no move one way or the other.

Massachusetts was strange and frightening, Bridie told herself with dismay, and the people who lived there were as well. Witches and wolves and savage heathen were abroad in the land, and the people who took them by the throat were perhaps just as dangerous. It was truly terrible to Bridie, as though cracks had opened up in the earth around to reveal glimpses of a bloody, brutal Hell. She began to shiver.

"Come, Bridget," her mother said, leading her away.

Bridie dragged her gaze off the wolf's head, saw the three Indians turn and slowly walk away inland, and allowed herself to be pulled into the square, plain meeting house.

Once inside, she was instantly caught up by the damp cold of the place. A chill like that of a tomb pervaded every corner despite the fact that the building was filled fore and aft with wool-clad worshipers.

"Do they not have a fire to warm the place?" Bridie

whispered to her mother as she sat meekly beside her parents in a pew and rubbed her aching hands together.

Mistress MacKenzie raised her eyes to the loft, and for one moment, Bridie was afraid fires were another strange custom that the Puritans' God frowned upon. But then her mother leaned close.

"The loft is where the gunpowder is stored. The meeting house is our garrison against the savages. The Naumkeag leave us be, but none can tell when the heathen might strike us. So we keep the powder here and may not dare to light any fire under it."

Without another word, Mistress MacKenzie slipped the mittens off her hands, and placed them in Bridie's lap with a brief smile. Then she turned to the minister.

In the pulpit, the Reverend Master Stoughton began to intone a prayer. Bridie heard hardly a word as she looked at the muskets lined up by the door. She closed her eyes, sending a prayer of her own to Saint Mary. She was cold.

But she made herself open her eyes and let her gaze travel slowly around the congregation of two hundred or more. She saw many more men than women, strange to say, but wives there were, and daughters and sons. Bridie saw two or three girls of her own age, and also the Carters. She hoped to take a word with her shipboard friends after the service, and hoped also that she would find new friends. She saw the sharp-faced Goody Handy and her son, and Goody Furness, who lived across Front Street from the MacKenzies, as well as other faces already slightly familiar.

In a pew near the wall, two small boys were taunting one another with turkey-feather quills. Bridie watched them, feeling a wary smile come to her face. A man in a cockade hat, carrying a long pole, edged along the wall toward them, but they were intent on their mischief and did not heed him. Then the beadle brought the knobby end of the pole down on the first boy's head with a resounding crack, and a startled yelp rang out in the cold air.

The minister paused for a moment in his sermon, shot the boys a stern look, and went on. Bridie covered her mouth with one hand to hide her smile, and felt somewhat better in her mind. Her eyes met those of another girl, and they shared a secret grin.

Smiling, Bridie lifted her head and looked around again. The folk of Marblehead listened dutifully to the sermon in the cold and cheerless room. They were patient.

And so would Bridie be. So she must be, regardless of how the Protestant words that came to her from the pulpit jarred against her Catholic heart. As the Reverend Master Stoughton exhorted the crowd, Bridie felt Mistress MacKenzie take her hand in a quick, hard clasp. The mother surely knew what a trial the daughter endured. Bridie felt a rush of gratitude and drew strength from being reunited with her family. That was surely worth sitting through any number of Protestant services.

At the noon hour, the sermon came to an end, and Bridie roused herself with a start. Her parents rose quickly, hurrying out of the meeting ahead of the congregation so as to make the ordinary ready for the men of the town. They fairly ran down Front Street, and Bridie felt a sense of relief and deliverance to be running from the cold and gloomy church.

"We've more menfolk here than many places," Master MacKenzie warned. "They come from Cornwall and Devon for the fish. They scarce stop work on the Sabbath as it is, and do require plentiful refreshing."

"Master Penworthy says they came here not for God, but for cod," John added.

His mother cuffed him. "Don't repeat such wickedness."

Bridie glanced behind her, sorry not to have had a chance to stop and meet the other girls of the town. She could see the congregation streaming away from the meeting house, and she scanned the crowd for the girl whose smile she had met during the long, tedious sermon. But Bridie's mother called to her impatiently.

"Bridie, get you into the cellar and draw a jug of ale," she said as they entered the house. "Folk will be here momently."

John was stirring the fire to life, and their father was plucking mugs from the shelves. It was the Puritan law's requirement that all ordinaries be sited near the meeting house for the convenient plenishment and rest of the men on the day when no work could be done. Bridie knew that a dry crowd was hard on the family's heels.

Pausing only long enough to hang her cloak on a nail, Bridie lifted the planks that hid the cellar hole. Down below, in a small space carved from the rock, stood barrels of ale. Bridie took the leather jug her mother held down to her and filled it from the bung hole. Even as the sweet, malty fumes rose up to her, she heard the door open and the tread of many footsteps and voices raised in greeting.

"Listening is dry work," one man joked. "Give us something to wash it down, Host. I have such a thirst I could almost drink water."

"I've been forced to it myself," another man declared in a tone of regret.

Bridie lifted the jug up to the floor, and pulled herself up the ladder into the noisy keeping room. The moment her curly-haired head appeared, a silence descended. The men crowding around the fire nodded at her, and then looked shyly away.

"Good day to you all," Bridie said in a friendly tone. She would match them. She would not let herself be frightened or dismayed by the newness and strangeness of everything around.

Some of the men looked to her and gave her smiles.

"Good day, Mistress MacKenzie," said a gruff, white-haired man with a face like tanned leather. He had taken the best seat nearest the fire and was heating a poker in the coals. "Give us a tankard, if you please."

There was a pause as Bridie went to fetch one of the pewter mugs. In her nervousness, she swept it off the shelf and onto the floor, where it bounced and clanged like a bell. The silence grew tighter.

"I vow only to spill the empty mugs," Bridie said.

The men laughed, and the room relaxed. Bridie filled the pewter tankard for the man at the fire, and the conversation welled up again and spilled into every corner. More and more men arrived, filling the room with their heat and noise and rough smells. In no time, Bridie was busily pouring ale and cider, greeting the patrons, and helping her parents. She could not help noticing as well how the younger men stood straighter as she passed and could not help smiling at their rough compliments.

"Welcome to Marblehead," a blond fellow said with easy gallantry. "We hope you have a taste for fish."

"And I hope you always have a taste for our brew," Bridie returned. She grinned and walked away as he and his mates exchanged pokes in the ribs.

Near the door, Master Carter stood awkward and ill at ease. Bridie carried a mug to him. "Thank you again, sir, for your services to me on our passage," she said.

He smiled. "My lassie is doing well, thanks to you."

"I did what I could, and Maggie did the rest," Bridie said. "Give her some dainties with her food, and she'll grow strong."

He nodded. "Come see for yourself how she does. My wife would thank you for a visit. This place is all strange and new."

"Don't I know!" Bridie smiled, comforted by the knowledge that she was not alone in finding Marblehead very different from home. "I saw you and your family at meeting," she added.

Master Carter sipped at his mug. "Aye," he said in a low voice. He glanced around cautiously. "My wife was much aggrieved to go. But here is where the work is, so go to meeting we must."

"Tell her I'll visit her soon," Bridie said, seeing her mother beckon to her. She hurried away.

"Bridie, Master Bowman desires a rum fustian," Mistress MacKenzie said breathlessly, taking a rare nutmeg and a grater from the press. "Take to him beer, sherry, the yolk of an egg, and the nutmeg. He'll flip it all with the poker."

Nodding, Bridie did as she was told and carried the brimming tankard to the white-haired man at the fireplace. With a rough word of thanks, he took the tankard and plunged in the red-hot iron poker he took from the coals. Instantly the liquid foamed and boiled into a steaming froth. Bridie laughed with delight.

"Flip it indeed," she said with a smile. " 'Tis flipped right over."

Master Bowman lifted the tankard and took a long pull, grinning over the rim from creased gray eyes. "Ah," he gasped. "That'll keep me warm for the afternoon service."

Bridie's smile fell. "Afternoon service?"

Her father nodded as he put another log on the crackling fire. "Tithing man will be here soon to hurry us back to meeting," he said. "Sabbath is only halfway done."

Sighing with resignation, Bridie went to fill emptied mugs. "Saint Bridget, give me strength," she muttered.

Two men standing near her stopped their conversation and looked at her in surprise.

"Master Carter!" her mother spoke up in a loud voice, stepping in front of Bridie and shielding her from

48

view. "We've not thanked you properly for looking after our daughter on the crossing."

Bridie's face was hot with embarrassment and confusion, and Master Carter looked highly uncomfortable at Bridie's mistake too.

"Aye," Master MacKenzie said. "We must not charge you for your ale."

"I thank you," Carter mumbled.

The men resumed their conversation, and Bridie let her breath out. "Forgive me, Mother," she whispered.

"I do. But you mun guard your tongue carefully, Daughter," Mistress MacKenzie said in an undertone.

Bridie swallowed hard. "I will from this time on."

Chapter Five

At the afternoon service, Bridie shared another smile with the girl she'd seen that morning. And as the service ended, they found themselves walking out together with the other females.

"You're Bridget MacKenzie, are you not?" the girl asked in a low voice. She was tall and willowy, with wheat-colored hair. "I'm called Sarah Furness."

Bridie wondered if speaking as they proceeded out was frowned upon and guessed it was. She was glad that Sarah had ventured to do it for her.

"Let us be friends, Sarah," Bridie whispered. "I would like that."

"My family lives only across from yours," Sarah said. "Come find me when you can."

Then Sarah was gone, walking with bowed head behind her mother and older sisters away from the meeting house. Bridie smiled. She'd indeed go looking for her new friend when she could. But for the moment, there was business again at the ordinary, and she hurried home with her family, thinking sadly of Kit in Scotland.

The following morning, Bridie set herself to see if the rose cuttings so hard cared for would take. Already she had taken notice of the wild roses that grew where the narrow, muddy streets dwindled into footpaths. She took a pick and dug one out and carried it back to the ordinary.

"What are you after?" her brother asked, seeing her attack the stony garden soil in the side yard with the pick.

"I'm grafting the slips I brought with me," she explained. "Johnny, fetch me a knife, do."

His green eyes met hers curiously, and then he shouldered open the door. In a moment, he was back, holding out a knife in his hand. He squatted near her in the dirt, watching her careful incisions in the bark.

"We'll soon see if these take," Bridie told him, tying the grafts in place with thin strips of leather. Her fingers worked deftly with the wet twigs, and she felt the sun press warm on her back. She looked around, and saw how firmly rooted the ordinary was to its rocky bed. Massachusetts was a place where all things could thrive. There was robust defiance wherever Bridie looked, and she valued the beauty it made of itself. She smiled and touched the grafts gently.

"Will they grow new on this plant?" John asked in wonderment. " 'Tis a marvelous thing to take dead sticks and make them live again."

51

"But they're not dead sticks," Bridie said. "The life's asleep down inside them, waiting to spring forth. Like all there is around us here."

She pointed to the small, new shoots of grass and plants that poked through the soil, and at a dauber wasp that crawled dazedly onto a sunny rock, opening its wings to warm itself in the pale sunlight. John looked at them, and then smiled up at her, his round face bright in the sun.

"Our grandfather knew all the care of roses and other plants," Bridie continued. "He taught me a muckle of lore. He was a goodly man, Johnny, and I miss him very much."

John poked into the wet earth with a stick. "Miss you Scotland too?"

"Ah . . ." Bridie bowed her head, thinking of the home she had left, of Father Dougal and his homely, earnest face, of Kit's sharp laughter when Bridie sang off-key to tease her, of the smell of peat fires and the rumble of cartwheels leaving, leaving . . .

"I do," she said with a sigh.

"But are you not happy to be with us here?"

"Certainly I am," Bridie said. She gave him a swift kiss on the top of his head. "I wouldn't ever want to leave you, but it was my home, you know. I must bump into a good many things here until I find how I fit."

He gave her a puzzled grin, seemed ready to say something, and then shook his head. "What do you know of plants?" he asked, turning back to a more sensible topic.

Bridie eased her back. "When I was your age, I knew a great deal already. I know the plants back home, and I'm hoping that many are the same here. But already I have seen scores of new plants. They grow from every cranny and patch of earth. I will go out later and see which ones I know."

"Do not stray too far," her mother said, overhearing Bridie from the doorway. "The Indians are always hard by."

"But didn't you say the Naumkeag were peaceable?" Bridie asked.

Her mother hugged her arms about herself and squinted at the sky. "They have been. But do not stray too far," she repeated, and she went back indoors with John following behind her.

Bridie was suddenly afire to be off alone, away from the new rules and strangeness of it all, away from the need to be always learning her way. She hastily wiped her hands on her apron and swept up her basket and cloak from beside the doorstep. Then, before anyone might tell her she was overstepping another line, she ran from the ordinary and out toward the rocky shore. She soon put the small town behind her. She'd search for plants and then come back and find Sarah Furness.

The breeze whipped her heavy skirts around her legs as she tramped up through the long, tawny tussocks of grass and stepped around lichenous boulders. Always to her right was the rising, heaving mass of the ocean, glittering and vast. She scrambled up onto a rocky outcropping and stood looking out at the sea, holding her balance

53

hard as the wind buffeted her. It was a magnificent prospect, full of light. Sails she could see out on the water and then the rolling slow arc of a whale's back as it crested far out and sounded the depths. Bridie felt awe take hold of her, and she held out her arms to embrace the great ocean.

Then a sudden gust snatched the basket from her hand and tumbled it to the grass. Bridie jumped down to chase it and felt with dismay that her hair was coming loose from its pins. For a moment, she stopped to catch the loose strands, but the basket gusted away again, and Bridie gave chase, laughing at the contrariness of the wind.

"What an unchancy wind," she gasped, swooping down on the basket before it could blow out of her reach again. She plumped down on the grass in a cuplike hollow, tucked one foot through the handle of the basket, and then addressed herself to her hair.

"Now you'll stay," she ordered it, her eyes gleaming and her cheeks rosy with the wind. She coiled her hair on her head, feeling for the pins that never seemed to hold it for long.

Then she stilled her hands, aware that she was not alone. Slowly she raised her eyes. A young man was standing at the rim of her grassy bowl, looking down at her in amazement. Bridie stared back at him, wondering what made him look so strangely at her. And then her hair tumbled down onto her shoulders again. Bridie giggled. She could not help it with the wild mood that was on her.

"What are you?" the young man said hoarsely, staring

at her as though she were a spirit. His fine features were pulled awry by uncertainty, and his blue eyes were wide with dismay.

Bridie's brows arched. "I am a MacKenzie, is what I am, Will of God Handy."

He looked even more alarmed. "You know my name."

"And you ought to know mine and who I am, for you've seen me with my mother as I've seen you with yours," Bridie retorted, amused by his dazed manner. She wrestled again with her wild, willful hair, and finally subdued it. She grasped the basket and stood up.

Will drew himself upright. "I am just returned from Salem," he said in a steady voice. "What do you here?"

"Learning this new land," she replied. " 'Tis many ways alike to Scotland—these rocks and hills, this sweeping wind. But also unlike."

"How?" He looked around as though the notion of learning the land was new to him.

Bridie tipped her face to the sky. "This light. This ocean here," she said, opening her arms wide again. " 'Tis very grand."

" 'Tis dangerous and full of evil," Will said stiffly. He drew a shaky breath, and then his brow cleared, and Bridie saw he was a handsome fellow when the look of solemnity left him. "What do you gather?"

"I search for herbs that might heal," Bridie told him, wishing for an instant that her hair might come down again to rattle him.

His frown returned. "If it be God's will that a man sicken, none should hinder it."

"What a hard thing to say!" Bridie gasped. "It surely is not God's will that we suffer without need? I know physics and simples that might cure an aching head or strengthen the blood and make a body well." She looked at him hard. "The better to do God's work. 'Tis nowhere ordained that we should not help the sick."

Will shook his head stubbornly. "God has His plan and should not be hampered."

"God's plan includes the plants He put here for our use," Bridie insisted, pointing out to the growing green all around.

"Nay."

"Och," Bridie gasped and brought her hand down hard by her side. Through the cloth of her skirt, she felt something sharp. Curious, she reached into her pocket and drew out the crooked nail she had picked up on the ship.

"Why do you carry such a talisman?" Will asked suspiciously.

"I don't carry it," she replied. "Not by design. Nor is it a talisman, but a simple nail. I only picked it up for thrift."

Will looked affronted. "A crooked nail may not be so simple."

"I believe the fairies have been at you," Bridie said, laughing. She tossed the nail away, only to shock and confound him more. "You're all mizzled in the head."

He flushed angrily, which tickled Bridie further. She

knew she should cease her taunting, but she could not. She also knew that he could walk away from her but did not, and it brought the color to her cheeks.

"And perhaps I'm the fairy that mizzled you," she went on, her eyes dancing. "Mayhap I've been sent by old Hornie himself to tempt you, as well."

"I know you jest, Mistress MacKenzie," Will said sternly. "But it is an evil thing to do."

Bridie laughed again. "Don't be so certain I do jest, for I may have powers you cannot reckon. The famousest seer of Scotland was a MacKenzie, you know, the Seer of Brahan from the Isle of Lewis. He could see the future through a hole in a little stone."

As Will looked on, dumbfounded, Bridie picked up a small rock and held it up. "They say he blint his eye by staring through the stone." She raised it to her eye.

"Don't!" Will exclaimed, and then flushed in embarrassment when she laughed.

Bridie had not enjoyed herself so much since she had left Scotland. The effect she had on Will Handy delighted her, and she cast about for some other means to bring that look to his face. Then she began to sing.

"O, rattlin' roarin' Willie, he held to the fair,
An' for to sell his fiddle, and buy some other ware
But partin' wi' his fiddle, the salt tear blint his e'e
And rattlin' roarin' Willie, ye're welcome home to me!"

Bridie tucked her basket under her arm, sent a smile to the shocked Will, and walked away.

"What a ramping fool," she said, chuckling.

But she thought she'd like to see him again.

She spent some time foraging for familiar plants and found some that looked the same as the ones she knew from home. These she gathered and placed in her basket, and then made her way back into the town. For a moment, as her new home came to view, Bridie stopped. The ordinary was as gray as the rocks around it. And yet, like the rocks, seemed to glow in the sunshine and give back a living warmth. She smiled and went toward it.

"Good day, Mistress," said a stoop-shouldered fisherman in a muffled voice as Bridie neared the ordinary.

Bridie nodded politely. "Master Trelawney, is it? How do you today?"

"Aye, Trelawney it is. And Trelawney does terrible bad with a toothache today," he grumbled. He twisted up his face and rubbed his jaw.

Bridie recognized him from the ordinary and remembered that he had been one who had heard her calling on her patron saint the day before. She was eager to appease him lest he doubt her readiness to follow the Puritan law.

"If it's a toothache you have, I can relieve it," Bridie told him. "Hold hard by."

She picked through the plants in her basket while the man shifted from foot to foot and gruffly cleared his throat to spit. Among her finds was the bark of the black haw, and she took the woody bits in her hand.

"Steep this in boiling water for some time, sir," she told the Cornishman. "It should take off a good bit of the pain until someone might pull the tooth."

He looked at the bark in her hand. "Oh, aye. And a sup of your father's ale will take off the pain, as well."

"Aye, sir," Bridie agreed. "And will topple you from your boat mayhap. Try this. Kitchen it with honey, and it will go down the easier."

He squinted at her doubtfully, but he held out his hand so that she could drop the pieces of bark into his palm. Then he stumped off down the street. Bridie watched him go. Queer, rough folk they were in Marblehead, but she would make a place for herself among them.

She squared her shoulders and picked her way across the muddy street to make her acquaintance with Sarah Furness.

Chapter Six

SARAH WAS SCALING fish in the side yard when Bridie put her head around the corner of the house. Sarah's arms below her rolled-up sleeves were red with blood and sparkling with the shiny glints.

"You're in a bloody business," Bridie said.

"Aye, I know it." The girl tossed aside the mackerel she had cleaned, wiped her fouled hands on her apron, and picked up another. The knife in her hand went *wink-wink-wink* in the sunlight, scattering shining scales in a rainbow shower. A striped cat waiting nearby for a morsel shook its head in surprise as scales rained down on it, then licked them carefully out of its fur.

"This town smells all of fish," Bridie commented. "I begin to wonder if you people aren't all fish yourselves."

Sarah laughed. "It could be. 'Tis true I know some proper fishwives in this town."

"And you have a fish called chub, do you not?" Bridie

asked, thinking of some of the portlier patrons she had seen at the ordinary. "I met some of them yesterday."

"Aye, and we've fish called maid." Sarah giggled, and brushed a stray filament of hair from her cheek, streaking it with fish blood. "Sheepshead too."

Bridie felt a laugh rise in her own throat. "I believe I met a sheepshead just now," she said, glancing back over her shoulder. "He goes by the name Will of God Handy."

"Will Handy!" Sarah pointed to the dull dead eye of a fish with her sharp knife. "This mackerel has more life in him than Will Handy does."

"Does he study to be a minister?" Bridie asked. "He's very solemn."

"He only studies to *act* the minister," Sarah said with a snort. "Why such questions?"

Bridie felt the color rise to her cheeks under Sarah's knowing look. "It is only . . . he—"

"Is a very comely fellow?" Sarah suggested. She grinned. "He is that and would be a good catch were it not for that harpy of a mother."

"She does seem . . . queer," Bridie said, hesitating over the right word for Goody Handy.

Sarah put down her knife and looked earnestly at Bridie. "I think it is worse than that. I once stopped to speak to Will, and his mother called me a harlot and a whore in front of the congregation." Sarah's own face colored angrily at the memory.

"No!" Bridie stared. "What had you said?"

Tossing her head, Sarah picked up her knife again

and attacked another mackerel with it. "Nothing worse than 'good day to you.'"

Bridie looked down, pleating her apron between restless fingers. "Those are no strumpet's words, surely. But did not Will of God—"

"There are plenty of other fellows just as handsome as he," Sarah said. "But with a mother like that, he's no catch for anyone. Give him a wide berth if you want to keep that woman's malice from you."

"You're not afraid of her, are you?" Bridie asked in surprise. "She's surely harmless even if she is queer."

Sarah tossed her head. "I'm never afraid of her. But why court such strife? Tell me, had you a sweetheart where you came from?"

"Nay, none," Bridie said with a blush. "It was a tiny, country place I lived in, and few men about for that."

"Then this is the place for you," Sarah said, grinning. "'Tis full of wifeless men come over for the cod. I'm glad you're here—it may be you'll draw some of the crowds from me so I'll have some breathing room!"

Bridie laughed out loud, glad to talk of girlish things again.

"Bridie? Bridie!"

Bridie started. "'Tis my mother. I must go."

Her new friend nodded and gave her a smile. "Remember, Bridie," she said quickly. "You may cast your net wide in this town. You needn't keep any fish that aren't to your liking or that leave a bad taste."

Bridie hurried away and called back over her shoulder. "I'll mind well what you've said, Sarah. I'll come see you again, soon."

She ran across the street to the ordinary, turning over Sarah's words in her mind. "I'm here, Mother," she said as she opened the door.

"You've visitors," Mistress MacKenzie replied.

Bridie spun around. Mistress Carter and little Margaret were seated on a bench near the fire.

"Well, look at this bonny lassie!" Bridie said with delight as the girl stood up. "This isn't the same poor sickling I tended on the ship, is it?"

Margaret ran to her, her cheeks rosy. "I am, I am."

Mistress Carter came forward and placed her hands on Margaret's shoulders. "She is nearly back to her romping ways," she said, looking down fondly at her daughter.

"So I can see," Bridie said. "This place has good air and sun. You'll soon be growing like a weed, Maggie."

"Aye, she eats enough for four." Mistress Carter laughed.

Margaret smiled. "We never had so much food in Scotland. We've had meat broth with every meal, haven't we, Mama?" She tipped her head back to grin at Mistress Carter.

"So we have, and so you shall keep on having if you like it, poppet."

Bridie's mother brought a mug of cider to the other woman with a smile. "And how do you find it here?" she asked. "I know it seems rough at first, but you'll become used to it as we did." She looked pointedly at Bridie as she spoke.

Mistress Carter glanced at Bridie also and then lowered her eyes. "My man is already hard at work with the other boatwrights," she said in a formal, polite voice. "And we are thankful for all the good things we find here."

"You're not sorry you came, then?" Bridie asked, recalling the woman's great fear and reluctance on board the *Rose*.

"Nay, nay!" Mistress Carter shook her head. "We'll prosper here. There were no such chances back in Scotland."

" 'Tis why we left, as well," Bridie's mother said.

"Come to our house, Bridget," Margaret said, tugging on Bridie's hand. "The windows have true panes in them."

Bridie laughed. "I can't now, sweeting, but soon, I promise."

"We must be getting home," Mistress Carter said. "Thank you again for your services to our daughter."

"And we thank you for the same," Bridie's mother replied.

Bridie saw them to the door and watched as they made their way up Front Street. The Carters were fitting themselves in, despite the constraints of the Puritan town, and soon Margaret might have no memory of another home but Marblehead. Bridie wished it could be as easy for her as it was for the girl. She closed the door and went back to work.

Over her first two weeks, life slipped into a routine for Bridie, filled with the work of brewing and distilling, baking, spinning and serving. Bridie soon learned that although Massachusetts was a rigorous, straitlaced Puritan colony, Marblehead remained a place to itself. The independent fishing town picked and chose among the many laws to suit its own pleasure and convenience. In consequence, the MacKenzie ordinary was busy every day in the week, and loud laughter and argumentation echoed within the great fireplace. Bridie saw that indeed there were more men than women in the town, and if her presence brought more of them than usual to her family's establishment, she was glad for it.

And when Bridie was not needed at home, she visited Sarah or roamed the seashore and the inland meadows about the town on the fine, blustery April days. With each outing, she saw more things to delight her, and she found herself growing to love the bright seaside light and the stark, wild beauty of the rocky shore. Once in her first week, to her surprise, she startled two Indian women collecting mussels from the low-tide rocks. Bridie's heart raced within her, but the women only smiled shyly and went on with their work. Bridie wished she could stay and watch them, to look long and carefully at their unusual clothing and dark, different faces, but she turned away. She was uncertain of the wisdom of tarrying near them, although they appeared harmless indeed. From then on she occasionally glimpsed Indians as she went here and there, but she could not bring herself to approach them, for they were pagans.

She also learned from her father how some of the Indian tribes had banded with the French to the north, and were harrying the English colonists throughout New England. Coastal adventuring by the French and Indians had hampered the fishing trade as well, and the fishing folk looked hard on all the Indians, whether allied with the French or not. So Bridie was cautious and kept her distance.

April burgeoned into May, and the sun drew scents from the earth that beckoned to Bridie from every direction, making her pause as she worked in the garden and breathe with a sense of anticipation. She stepped outside at the noontime one day, judged she did not need a wrap, and walked out carrying a basket with John's meal. He and the other boys of the town kept watch over the fish flakes every day, keeping away the birds that screamed for food to fill their rocky nests and the keening chicks. Bridie took the path to the beach, warming her face in the sun, and soon came upon her brother and a fellow of his among the fluttering whirl of birds. They were flapping their arms and practicing at skipping rocks along the waves.

The sun blazed, and the smell of drying cod was strong enough to flavor broth. John ran to Bridie when he spied her and sat down hungrily to his meal. Perched on a rock beside him, Bridie watched her brother eat, knowing that he had a strong hold on her heart already. She smiled at him.

"The saints are surely watching over you, bonny boy."

He squinted up at her in the dazzling light. His form was silhouetted by the white cloud of gulls and terns. "Be the saints like these birds, then?" he asked with full mouth. "Flying about overhead?"

"Perhaps they are," Bridie said with a laugh. She ruffled his hair and plucked up the basket to return home by another path. She was smiling, humming to herself, and thinking of her brother, when she came upon a dark and crabbed-looking house.

It was the Handy ordinary, she knew. She'd not glimpsed Will of God since the first time except at meeting, although Goody Handy was often seen stumping by, scowling at all and sundry. Bridie was curious to know what trade the MacKenzies' rival managed at this gloomy, unwelcoming place, where the door stood in chill shadow and the greedy gulls shrieked overhead like lost souls.

As Bridie paused to glance at the house, she heard a flustered clucking from above. She raised her eyes and saw Will standing on the roof by the chimney, a scolding hen under his arm. Will was standing still and gaping down at her as he had at their first meeting, with a startled look in his vivid blue eyes. Outlined against the sky above her, he was like a painting Bridie had once seen of Saint George, beautiful and brave, as he slew the dragon.

All at once, Bridie's heart began knocking hard within her, and she felt the heat rise to her cheeks. They stared at one another thus for some few seconds. Even in such a roost, Will managed to look as solemn and serious as a minister, and Bridie itched to topple his respectability.

"You'll never teach her to fly if she does not already know," she said after a moment.

Will gaped at her dumbly and then recalled the hen under his arm. It clucked again in anger as he tightened his grip.

" 'Tis only to clean the chimney," he said. He turned away and stuffed the bird down the stone flue. Bridie could hear its squawking as it plummeted downward, raking and sweeping the soot as it went. Will stood there, irresolute and empty-handed.

"And can you fly even if the poult cannot?" Bridie taunted.

Will shook his head and suddenly lost his balance with a cry. Bridie's hands went to her face as he slithered down the shingled roof, fell onto the lean-to shed, and then slid off into the mud near some swine. The shed wobbled slightly in the silence.

For a moment, Bridie stood aghast. But then the sight of the dignified Will sitting in the offal overcame her, and she burst into a peal of merry laughter. Will glowered at her in embarrassment.

"I'm sorry," Bridie said the next instant, stepping forward with hands outstretched. "Are you hurt?"

"No." As Will drew himself up from the mud, a piglet trotted over to smell his foot and then squealed.

Bridie broke into laughter again, and Will joined her with a rueful grin. "He must think me a new brother," Will said as he pushed the curious piglet away.

"If you will wallow in the mud with him, what else should he think?" Bridie teased, hardly able to look at him without her heart racing again. Even spattered and grimed as he was, Will was still as handsome a young man as she'd ever known. And in truth, she liked him even better in the mud if it made him smile. She risked raising her eyes again to his face and felt the wild rushing inside her as before.

"How do you find it here?" Will asked. "Still strange to you?"

"Still strange indeed, but I find it very good for all that," Bridie said, meeting his eyes steadily.

The door of the ordinary was flung open at that time, and there stood Goody Handy with another sour and black-eyed goodwife beside her. They stared at Bridie with undisguised hostility.

"Good day," Bridie said, nodding her head and hoping her look was a modest one.

They did not return her greeting. Goody Handy's eyes were black and hard and unblinking and seemed to grow more so with each moment.

"What has she done to you?" the woman demanded of her son.

"She's done naught," Will replied, his manner instantly serious and proper again. "I only fell." He brushed some of the mud off his clothes and went into the shed without another word.

"Mistress," Bridie began, wishing to soothe Goody Handy and mindful of Sarah's warning words. "Mistress, I only—"

"Stay away," Goody Handy spat.

A shiver went up Bridie's back as she met the woman's baleful look, and she felt something uncanny and fearsome as a tangible force. Not knowing what else to do, she walked quickly away.

"Queer old hoodie-crow," she said under her breath. She shook herself to be rid of the coldness of Mistress Handy's eyes, but it seemed to linger like a mist.

She quickened her steps and was soon back on Front Street at the door of her family's place. She let herself in.

The usual crowd of men was there, the hard-laboring fishermen who stayed out for days at a time and came in at odd intervals to eat hot meals and warm their spirits with ale and rum. Bridie went to assist her mother.

"I just came past Goody Handy's," she said quietly. "The woman stares at me as though I'd sprung horns."

Her mother nodded. "Be on guard for her. She's as dour as seven ministers, and not a drop of charity in her. She'd have us before the magistrate if there were a law against prosperity."

"Do you think she's not right in the head?" Bridie asked.

"Don't ask me that, I don't know," Mistress MacKenzie said. "But it does seem she watches her son like she feared he'd fly away if he goes out of her sight."

"I've a song for her next time I see her," Bridie said, grinning as she retied her apron. " 'O Willie brewed a peck o' malt—' "

"Hush with that clishmaclaver!" Mistress MacKenzie scolded, pushing Bridie away with a smile and looking to see if any of the men had heard Bridie's song. All were busy with argument, though, and did not hark to the women.

Bridie took a full flagon of ale to the men and listened to their debate.

"I say I have seen the creatures with my own eyes," Trelawney declared, striking his tankard on the scarred table. "The sea do be full of such unnatural things."

"It may be the sea is more full of unnatural things after you've had your fill of ale," Penworthy said, laughing.

Master Bull, whose form and manner accounted well with his name, rubbed one hand over his seamy face. "Aye. But leave that alone and be not so free to talk of unnatural things. The sea is full enough with natural creatures, the leviathan, the giant squid that takes a ship entire."

"A ship entire, Master Bull?" Bridie asked.

"A ship entire. Aye!" Bull insisted as a chorus of protest went up. "There's many and many a queer thing that happens at sea!"

Bridie took up a pestle and began pounding sweet dried pumpkin into a powder to flavor switchel. Her hands rose and fell rhythmically as she gazed at the man. She had already learned that these people, living in such reliance on the vast, terrible sea, were strongly moved by its mysterious power. All held it in great awe.

A shriveled, weatherworn man held up his hand. "Queer indeed! Look to the Deliverance of God from the whirlpool and the hurricano. Take any three vessels at the same point at the same time, and two will go down but not the third. None can say that is not a judgment."

Trelawney snorted into his ale. "If we talk of judg-

71

ments, it does strike uncommon strange that Marblehead be not swallowed into the sea!"

There was laughter at that, but the solemn Bull did not join in. "Queer things do happen on the sea, but no queerer than what may happen on land."

Trelawney laughed again, elbowing his neighbor. "They say the magistrates in Salem deemed Marblehead too full of the Devil to take on, in the recent tribulations."

Bridie's ears pricked up at that. She stilled her hands, the better to listen. The great purge of witches had reached its peak only a few years earlier, and news had traveled even to Arrochar.

"The Reverend Mather asked if there were witches here," Bridie's father agreed. "But none were named."

"The folk by Salem think us all ungodly witches, but they could not try and hang the whole town," Penworthy barked, and laughed in his sunburned nose as he took a swallow of ale.

Bridie looked with interest from one man to the next. They spoke lightly of it. Perhaps they were too close to the might and careless whim of the ocean to be cowed by any power of man—or of the Devil.

"But they did try and hang witches in Salem?" Bridie spoke up, unable to keep quiet any longer. "Even in Scotland we heard news of the trials."

"Indeed, many were tried and hanged," her mother replied carefully.

"But were they truly witches?" Bridie pressed.

Several voices rose at once, clamoring for the loudest

opinion. Master Bull quieted them by pounding on the table.

"The Devil has been abroad in Massachusetts, and there's no denying it," he roared. "He strides here and there, picking his favorites as he goes. No doubt many of those hanged were wicked indeed."

"John Proctor was a strong and brave man," Penworthy said. His jocular manner was subdued, and he hunched his narrow shoulders unhappily. "I'll never believe him a warlock if the Devil himself comes and tells me so."

"But some confessed! There were witches that did confess," Bull said, glowering.

Bridie's father leaned his elbows on his knees, and shook his head at the fire. "Confessed under torture . . ."

"Confessed before the magistrates, in the presence of God and witnesses," Bull said. "Not under torture."

MacKenzie shrugged, but did not speak.

"Nay, but what do you make of that Tituba, the Negress from the Barbadoes?" Trelawney challenged the company with a sharp look. "I myself saw her once at Salem. They say she knew all manner of strange arts."

"Arts to heal—*and* to strike a body down from afar," Bull agreed.

Bridie blinked in sudden alarm. "Arts to heal? But these surely are not wicked arts."

"Some say she learned some black arts from the Naumkeag," Penworthy offered with a wink to stir up trouble. "I have heard some say the sagamores use all manner of plants and animals when their people sicken. It sounds devilish to me."

Opinions varied on that. Bridie was hurt to see that Trelawney offered no thanks for the relief she'd given him for the toothache, nor offered any opinion at all on the usefulness of herbal medicine. He glanced sidelong at her as the discussion heated, and she suddenly felt the hair on her arms prickle up. Her pulse skipped in warning.

Trelawney chose a pause to add a word. "They say that the sagamores call their demons during the cures, and that Tituba called on familiar spirits." He gazed down into his tankard. "They say she died calling their names. Mayhap they were names of saints, who may know?"

Bridie kept her gaze firmly on the floor. It was all she could do not to rise up and rail at him, for there was no question he was suggesting bad doings about her, drawing a line between herself and the heathens. And to link the saints to the sin of witchcraft was more than she could stomach. She knew the man had heard her call on her own special saints, and it made a bitter taste in her mouth to hear Trelawney use it against her.

Her mother came to her quickly and took away the mortar of dried pumpkin. "I want something from up above," Mistress MacKenzie said evenly. She pressed Bridie's back with both hands. "Go you up there to fetch it."

Bridie left without even asking what it was her mother desired. She hurried away and climbed up the wooden ladder to her retreat. Once there, she sat on the edge of her bed, hugging her arms about herself.

"Wicked, thankless man," she whispered. She shivered although the room was warm.

Then she caught sight of her old poppet down beside the bedstead where John had dropped it. She took it up and ran her thumb over its crudely carved features, gentling herself until her heart could slow down.

Scattered words came up to her through the floorboards, but she would not listen. Instead she looked about for a way to busy herself and drive Trelawney's insinuations from her mind. She dove into her dwindling store of herbal cures and sorted through the packets. Her fingers shook. One packet fell to the floor.

As she bent to retrieve it, the conversation below came even louder to her ears. She kneeled on the floor, listening.

"Papists too." That was Bull's rumbling voice. "Catholics may be worse than Quakers."

"Aye, calling on demons and worshiping idols too, I have heard." That speaker was Penworthy. "And the ruler of them all is that devil Pope in Rome."

The heat washed up Bridie's back, leaving her skin prickling. She could not abide that they were speaking that way. But rather than fly down in anger and perhaps land her family in great peril, she stayed where she was, kneeling, and covered her face to pray.

But she made her prayer silent even as the hateful words came piercing up through the cracks in the floor.

Drawing a steadier breath, Bridie reached for the dropped packet. It caught on a splinter and tore open, and before she could act, a handful of powdered sage sifted down through the floorboards onto the men below.

Bridie gulped. There was a startled silence in the room beneath her, and then a frenzy of sneezing filled the ordinary. For an agonized moment, Bridie struggled between fear and laughter. A shocked laugh forced through her lips, and she pushed herself to her feet and ran to the ladder.

"I beg your pardon," she exclaimed, hurrying back into the main room. "It was my clumsiness again."

The men gathered there turned and regarded her suspiciously.

"What mischief was this?" Bull demanded, getting lumberingly to his feet. "What have you put onto us?"

"It was only sage," Bridie said, amused by their worried frowns. "It can't hurt you."

"So say you," Penworthy muttered, shaking the dust from his wiry red hair and beating it from his clothes.

Trelawney was rubbing his eyes hard enough to make them water, and he looked blearily at Bridie. "If aught comes of this, maid . . ."

Bridie fought hard to keep the smile from her face. It was too ridiculous to believe. But the longer Trelawney stared at her, the more uneasy she became. "Sir, as I say, it was only sage," she repeated with a dry throat.

"And who knows what dark properties sage might have in certain hands?" Trelawney asked with a broad gesture. He pointed at Bridie. "I'll remember this if any mischance befalls me."

She stared at him in horrified disbelief. "But sir—"

Bridie's mother hurried to appease the men. "A foolish girl's clumsiness is all," she explained breathlessly. "Good men, take another tankard to wash it away."

"Nay, I'll not stay." Trelawney stumped out, banging the door behind him.

"And that's the first time he never stayed for a gift of ale," Penworthy muttered, his good nature nearly restored.

Bridie stared blankly at the door Trelawney had just slammed. Her mother stepped close to Bridie and dropped her voice to a whisper. "Have done with all that," she warned harshly. "Or you'll be the ruin of us all."

Stunned, Bridie watched her mother as she hurried to soothe the ruffled feathers. Then, with tears stinging her eyes, Bridie ran from the room.

Chapter Seven

BRIDIE WAS IN the garden, tending to the plants. Beside her rosebush there were vegetables started and also the common herbs for the still-room: lavender, thyme, hyssop, and others. Some of the beans were new to Bridie, as well as the squashes and gourds which she'd planted in mounds according to her mother's direction. She had asked for the whole plot to be given into her charge, and she spent each morning there, with her hands in the ever-warming dirt. Tender shoots were poking up into the air, moistened by the mist that came in off the water and heated by a sun that shone every day. In the garden, the balminess was not so different from the western coast of Scotland and Bridie forgot she was ever homesick, forgot she had herself been transplanted into a wild and unpredictable place. Even after a month in Marblehead, she still felt she must pick her way with caution: the roads and the ground were dry enough, but she did sometimes believe she might sink into a treacherous bog of Puritan rules.

Humming softly, she broke off last year's dead stalks from a stand of tansy, and then wiped the sweat from her brow. The plants seemed to grow without effort, basking in the shelter of the ordinary's shingled walls. In her fancy, Bridie imagined she could hear them straining upward from the fertile ground. She thought of poor barren Scotland and how hard the folk there toiled for their meager harvests. Small wonder people came to the New World, then.

Bridie heard a soft whistle behind her and turned to see Sarah waving at her from the tiny window across the street. Sarah gestured and pointed and then put one finger to her lips. Puzzled, Bridie made as though to stand up, but Sarah shook her head. With an expectant smile, Bridie bent to her gardening again and waited to see what would happen.

Only a few moments later, the scrape of a bootheel on stone made her turn again. Will Handy was standing on the other side of the wattle fence.

"And how long have you been standing there?" Bridie asked, keeping back her smile. She could see Sarah still watching them with glee. "Do you not have anything better to do than peeking and spying?"

Will shook his head to protest, but his blushes gave him the lie. He'd been watching her, no doubt, but wouldn't own up to it. "I was not peeking and spying, Mistress MacKenzie."

"Then pray tell me, sir," she said, unable to keep from grinning wide, "what do you here?"

"I go to Salem with a charge from my mother," he explained stiffly. His blue gaze strayed constantly about her features, and then away. Bridie saw his throat working, tan and strong in the neck of his shirt. "I thought to ask if your family needs aught from there. They say the *Flying Mary* has put in from the Indies with a cargo of spices. Nutmegs and ginger even."

Bridie was suddenly sorry to have teased him so much, for now she could hardly speak without taunting him into cold haughtiness. He had come in earnest, desiring to do a favor to her, and she was flattered. Now she wished they might speak plainly, and that he would smile again as he had in the pig wallow. She also wished that her friend were not watching.

"I thank you, Master Handy," she said in a gentler voice. "To come out of your way to ask me—"

"I—I *don't* come out of my way," Will stammered. "But only into yours by chance. Nor do I ask *you*, but your family—"

"Och, Saint Kilda! You're as stiff as an aiken board, Will Handy," Bridie shot back at him. She turned her back and went back to her weeding. She scarcely saw what she pulled out, so strong was her botherment.

"And you're as muddy as a lobster. *And* as pinching."

Bridie's face burned. "Fly off to your *Flying Mary*, then. I don't want anything."

Will stood there for one more moment and then went away. Bridie peeked from under her tumbling-down hair as he made his way up the street. As soon as he'd turned the corner, Bridie flew into the house and up to her room. Once there, she took out her mirror.

"Och, no!" she wailed, holding it at arm's length and turning herself to and fro before it. A smear of mud was streaked across her forehead, and a dead leaf clung to her hair. She tossed the tiny looking-glass onto the bed, whipped off her apron, and scrubbed furiously at her dirty face and hands.

The next time Will Handy saw her, she vowed, she would *not* look like a lobster. She'd make certain of that.

But whether she pinched or no was not so certain. Smiling to herself, she went back down to finish her gardening.

"Bridget." Her mother's voice caught her at the door.

"Yes?"

Mistress MacKenzie was at the hearth, stirring something in a pot hanging on the crane over the fire. The wide fireplace pulsed with heat, and her mother's face was red with it. She turned her head to look at Bridie, and her features were crimsoned by the glowing flames. An odd fancy struck Bridie, catching her by the throat, that so would a person look—burning. She crossed herself without thinking.

"Bridie, no!" Mistress MacKenzie came quickly forward, and the lurid image was gone. She shook her head. The lines of worry about her eyes wrenched Bridie's heart. "No more crossing. You must put such ways behind you. We might lose everything if anyone chooses to make mischief."

Bridie, still startled by the picture she'd had of her mother, could only nod. Such hard work, such care, such sorry strife: those were what had drawn the lines in Flora MacKenzie's face and streaked the once-black hair with gray. Her parents had struggled hard and bitterly for their ordinary, given up much.

"Envy and covetousness are everywhere," Mistress MacKenzie said, taking one of Bridie's hands in her own. "We hold our license from the Governor, but he knows us not. There are folk who might find ways to reach his ear and tell him lies against us."

"But, Mother," Bridie said. "Marblehead is not strict about any laws that I can see—these people do care much more of cod than of God."

"That may be. But trade is trade. If it serves them to follow the laws for their own gain, so it might be. Anywhere else and you'd have been in the stocks by now, my girl! Don't you know that?"

Staring, Bridie shook her head. "But why?"

"For your faith." Mistress MacKenzie went back to stirring the pot over the fire. Her shoulders sagged, and when she spoke again she spoke quietly and into the flames. "Understand this, Bridie. You canna be *Catholic* and live here."

Bridie rebelled. "What harm do I do? And what can they do to me, who dislike it?"

In a whirl, her mother rounded on her and grabbed her by both arms. Her face was fierce. "They can send you right the way back to Scotland. This they do in Boston and Newtown, Salem—through the length of Massachusetts Colony, month by month."

"And so you would have me live here in deceit and heresy." Bridie pulled her arms free and turned her face away from her mother's gaze. She drew her breath shudderingly. "Better I should be sent back to starve in Scotland than fill my belly with such lies."

"Don't be foolish, Bridie!"

"But Mother—"

John burst in just then, full of noise and salty brashness, and bringing in the sea air. "I've found turtle's eggs," he cried out, his eyes shining in the dark room. "They're very fine, Bridie, from the giant turtle of the ocean. Have you ever tasted them?"

Bridie could not answer. She ached at the sight of her brother, so small and full of joyfulness. Be sent back to Scotland and never see him again? Be sent away when the whole will of her last ten years had been bent on coming to this place?

While he unloaded the store of eggs nested in his shirttail, he chattered on about finding them and digging them out with the shell of a clam. His voice carried into each corner of the room, skipping between mother and daughter as they looked at one another silently. His light laugh rang out, rollicking about Bridie's heart like a heedless, leaping dolphin.

"I will, Mother," Bridie said at last. "I'll put it all away."

But she was short of breath and not sure if she wanted to hold her brother or run away from the heartbreak that losing him would cause. Ducking her head, she left the house and ran down the street to the water.

She could not leave Marblehead, she thought, staring forlorn at the waves. In spite of the strangeness of its people, she already loved the beauty of it, already loved living within sight and sound and smell of the living ocean. And here was where her family was. Nor could she persist in her faith if it risked harm to her parents, her brother. It wasn't right that she should cling to it so if it could only bring ruin and despair to the ones she loved. She yearned to speak with Father Dougal, though, or some wise counselor.

But there was no one to talk to of such things.

"Bridie—what's amiss?" came Sarah's voice. She had followed Bridie down, and her normally white skin was flushed with running. "I saw you fly out of the house so fast!"

"I find it hard to breathe sometimes," Bridie said, closing her eyes and filling her lungs. She shook her head. "Is even the air made of different material here?"

"You're talking in riddles." Sarah put her hand on Bridie's arm. "What troubles you?"

Bridie turned bleak eyes to her friend. "Here I am with my family, and I love them. But I don't feel a part of them always. I feel separate, as though I still stood on the other side of the ocean." She gazed at the water and added softly, "I did think it would be otherwise."

"Now, Bridie, hush," Sarah said. "It's not long since you arrived. You will find your way among us. I know it."

Warmed by her friend's words, yet still sad, Bridie nodded. "Perhaps."

"You will indeed, and no halfhearted 'perhaps.'" Sarah gestured to the crooked maze of a town that clambered around the rocks on all sides. "Look around. There are no straight lines here. We go this way, and then the other, and then double back again. It confuses all newcomers. Don't lose faith."

"Faith . . ." Bridie stole a glance at her friend, and then turned her gaze back to the leveling ocean. She readied herself, and then spoke. "Do you know I'm Catholic?"

Sarah stepped backward involuntarily as a flush deepened across her face. "But—you go to meeting on the Sabbath."

"I do because I must." Bridie looked to see if Sarah would draw away from her now. Her faith had been a secret, as she'd known it must be. But she could not bear to feel so cut off. She wanted someone born in Marblehead to know. She wanted someone to acknowledge her. Lifting her chin, she watched her friend, waiting for the blow to fall and readying herself to bear it.

Sarah was looking at her with unmasked apprehension. "I had heard that Catholics were devilish," she said falteringly. "And practiced all manner of evil things."

"Am I devilish?" Bridie asked. "Have you known me to practice any evil at all?"

"No," Sarah admitted, her forehead puckered. "I do feel you are a good and godly person." She nudged a broken shard of clamshell with the toe of one shoe. "But yet . . ."

"Yet what?" Bridie asked hotly.

"I do not know." Sarah shook her head. "Does it hurt very much? To go to our meeting?"

At once Bridie's defiance melted, and tears sprang to her eyes. "It does, aye," she whispered. She struggled hard to find her voice. "You don't shun me for it, then?"

"I never knew a Catholic before," Sarah replied evasively. "There are many of them north, in New France, they say. Be Catholics all like you?"

Bridie drew one hand across her cheek, slowly shaking her head while she thought. "I do not know how the French are. But I know Catholics are no more like to one another than Puritans are. And even so, there is not so much difference between Catholics and Puritans as some say."

"Aye, I see your meaning," Sarah agreed. She frowned at the water. "I'm no philosophizer, but it seems to me that many folk here profess one thing and act another. It's only a way of fitting in."

Bridie gripped Sarah's arm. "That's true! I only act that way, and it is so false! I cannot abide by doing it!"

"But Bridie—" Sarah hastily eased her arm from Bridie's grip and sent a nervous glance over her shoulder. "You must abide by it, even so. You're back safe with your family now, and that must surely be worth being false on the outside."

"I believe so, and yet I don't," Bridie said. She was tired and confused and anxious, and wearily pushed her hair from her brow. "I must be like my rose cuttings. Here am I grafted now, and must adapt myself to a new climate or wither away."

"Yes," Sarah replied with keen relief. " 'Tis very like that. 'Tis what all do, I'm sure of it, for all must have at least one odd notion or another that does not suit well with his neighbor's and is covered up for appearance's sake. Only learn to seem one of us, and you will thrive."

"I'll make it my study, Sarah, if you'll help me," Bridie said.

"There, then it is done." Sarah let out her breath with a smile. "And soon you'll learn to put aside those popish practices in earnest and learn to follow God truly as we do."

Bridie blinked, her heart in her throat. Sarah did not shun her but did still believe that Bridie's faith was wrong. Inside, Bridie felt lorn and lone yet again.

"Come," Sarah said, linking her arm with Bridie's and steering a course back up from the water.

Bridie felt as confused as ever. But at the least, Sarah knew the truth about her and kept her as a friend. For the rest, Bridie could only hope she could learn to adapt, and pray that her faith would not wither away in the Puritan glare.

As they came around the corner, she saw a woman ahead struggling to push a cow along the path. The beast had planted its feet stubbornly, and all Bridie could see was the woman's bent back as she put her shoulder to the cow's tail.

"Can I help, Mistress?" Bridie asked, determined to

put herself in favor wherever she could. She was too late to see Sarah shaking her head.

The woman turned. It was Goody Handy. She looked Bridie up and down so coldly that Bridie felt a chill.

"I don't need your help," Goody Handy said. "Stay away." She picked up a stick and jabbed at the cow's haunch. With a lurch and a bellow, the animal moved forward at an ungainly trot, and Goody Handy marched after it.

Bridie felt as though she'd been struck or indeed jabbed with the stick as the cow had been. Such blatant scorn was impossible to ignore.

"Why does she use me so harshly?" she gasped.

Sarah made a sour face. "There's no reason but her own wicked heart," she said bitingly. "It's as I said before. She's ever cold and cruel to anyone her son takes notice of. Don't disturb yourself over such a one as that."

Bridie shuddered. "Oh, keep me strong," she said. "I'm trying."

Sarah looked off in the direction that the Widow Handy had gone and slowly shook her head. "Those Salem folk are a dour lot. Pay her no mind."

"Aye," Bridie whispered. But she could not ignore such an ill will, for it chilled her to the marrow of her bones.

There was much laughter that night as the ordinary filled with fishermen. Bridie kept to herself, serving and carrying but not speaking or humming her tunes. She could not help feeling as though she stood in a glare of light, working at the ordinary as she did. The town might come and look at her whenever it wished, and she could not escape its eyes. It made her feel open and vulnerable. Further, what Sarah had said to her saddened her deeply, for she feared that perhaps she would lose her true faith, as her parents had.

"The lass is uncommon quiet this night," Master Bowman said none too softly to Bull. "This modesty in her is very seemly, but not so merry as her manner was."

Bridie flushed, but continued to pour. Two fishing brothers, quiet Cornish lads who lived together, gave her their bravest smiles. But she dropped her eyes and would not return the same. Master Carter came in and nodded a greeting to her before taking a seat. The talk drifting among the men, ebbing and flowing like water, was of fish, of boats, of weather, of the French. Bridie heard more than one fisherman make idle boasts of driving the French out of the fisheries. But the fish were indeed so plenty that it hardly seemed to Bridie to be worth fighting for, when any boat could bring in a full catch at any time.

There was a commotion at the door, and Trelawney stumbled in, his boots foul with mud. "Ale, Host," he called to Bridie's father.

He sat on a bench by the fire and rubbed his neck with one dirty hand, mumbling angrily and shifting his weight as though the seat were too hot or too cold.

"And what makes you so sour?" Penworthy demanded, thumping him on the back. Trelawney coughed loud and hard.

"Only what ought to," Trelawney said with a scowl for his mate. "That sow that was delivered of ten piggies—didn't she take on an inflammation? And did she not just die of it?"

"Hard times, Trelawney," Master Bull said. He nodded judiciously. "And did you try—"

"I tried kicking her," Trelawney broke in. "But even that would not raise her."

Bridie poured cider into a jug for her mother and glanced back over her shoulder at the man.

"It all goes wrong with Trelawney," Mistress MacKenzie said in a low voice to Bridie, her mouth turned down with scorn. "He's a brute of a man and often as not is drunk. He's no more notion of caring for his beasts than does a lobster."

"I look to my enemies," Trelawney grumbled on. "There's many a one jealous of me."

Laughter burst out at this, and he glared.

"And who might be jealous of a boat that leaks, lines that break, and hooks that haul more weed than cod?" Bowman demanded of the room at large. He slapped his knee heartily at his own wit, and Bridie hid a smile.

"I say that sow never had any pox or inflammation *before* this," Trelawney said.

"Before *what*?"

Master MacKenzie's voice cut through the others. Bridie became slowly aware that some men were looking —or trying not to look—at her, and she felt a chill. Her father stared hard at Trelawney, and the man slowly dragged his gaze away and scowled at the fire.

"Before ever," he muttered into his drink.

Her heart racing, Bridie pulled her mother by the hand through the crowd and pushed open the door to the private room.

"What did he mean?" she asked in disbelief. "What do they say about me?"

"Nothing, nothing," her mother said, shaking her head. "Dinna listen to Trelawney, for he's a sour, scraping wastrel of a man and doesn't know what he means."

Bridie swallowed a lump in her throat. "But the others. There were others looked at me when he spoke of enemies—and pox. Do they think I might do such a mischief?"

"Nay, nay." Mistress MacKenzie cupped Bridie's cheek with one hand. Her eyes were sorrowing. "Be meek. Do not talk unless someone addresses you. Do not ramble the foreshore and woodlines like the idle, aimless Indians. Suit yourself to our ways, and they'll all see you for what you are—a good, comely girl with no harm in her."

Bridie pressed her face into her mother's warm hand and closed her eyes. She wished she might be a tiny child again. Life in Scotland had always been hard, but there had never been such dark, unquiet fears in her heart there, only the bright, stark fears of hunger and cold. Now she yearned to trade the blazing logs and plentiful stews for a pale peat fire and an oaten cake if it also meant vanquishing these whispering suspicions. Marblehead had much to offer; Marbleheaders had the power to withhold much too.

"The folk here are easily frightened," her mother said

91

in a sad voice. "Life is full of mischance and danger, and they are quick to fix blame where they can. I tell you this to save you from harm."

"Yes, Mother. I can see that." Bridie could feel the fear her mother felt for her. But she could not yet see how to change herself into something new.

"Go see your friend Sarah," Mistress MacKenzie suggested. "Or the Carters. See how little Maggie does."

"Yes . . . I will step outside for a while," Bridie said, clutching her mother's hand to her for another moment. Then she pushed away and went out the back door.

The night was early, and the air still held the warmth of afternoon, although the evening winds were gusting off the water. Bridie pressed herself into the shadow of the house by the garden and tried to steady her breathing. Loud laughter sounded through the wall behind her and carried into the darkness.

She bent over to touch the rosebush. It was flourishing, and in the dark she could feel the tender new leaves that the grafts were putting out. The ordinary was a warm and nourishing place, and her rose was well suited to thrive there, perhaps better suited than she. Shivering in spite of the warmth, she stood up and let herself out of the garden.

Her footsteps carried her along the rocky paths, where cats slipped through shadows and mice died. Here and there a light showed at a window, but the folk of the town mostly went to bed with the sun in order to be out in their boats before dawn. Bridie made no noise as she walked, her head bowed and her arms clasped around her for warmth. At one glowing window she paused and saw a man mending a net by the light of his fire, the hand shuttle plying in and out among the knots like a darting fish. Bridie hurried on.

Her knock sounded loud on the door of the Carters' house, a house still called Pittmans' for the last owner. A faint light showed in the cracks around the door's edge, and then Bridie heard a footstep.

"Who is it?"

"Bridget MacKenzie."

The door yawned open, and Mistress Carter's face showed luminously in the dark. "Bridget? Is aught amiss? Is my man drunk?"

Bridget shook her head. "Nay, Mistress. I only wanted to speak with you for a few moments, and then I'll be going home."

"Welcome, then." The woman stepped aside and ushered Bridie into the house. The fire on the hearth was the only light. In a truckle bed in one corner, Margaret lay with the covers pulled up to her chin, but she sat up when she saw Bridie lower herself onto a bench.

"Bridie!" she sang out. She flung the blanket back and padded forward on bare feet and helped herself to Bridie's lap.

"What a heavy weight you're becoming," Bridie said, bouncing the little girl on her knee. "Soon you'll be so big I'll be sitting in your lap."

Over Margaret's head, Bridie looked at Mistress Carter, and the older woman smiled. "She is growing apace and learning letters, too, from a hornbook."

"Nay!" Bridie looked into the young girl's eyes. "I never learned them myself. Mayhap you'll teach me. I saw your father at our ordinary, and he says his business goes well."

"My father builds boats," Margaret said proudly. "For the fishermen."

Mistress Carter poked at the fire. "I was afraid to remove to here from Scotland, but I'm nothing but glad for it now. And you see Maggie thrives." She laughed. "I believe she'll turn into a fish, the way she plays by the water."

"So you like the water then, you little otter?" Bridie asked.

"Yes, I do. I like to look for shells." The child's voice was heavy with sleep, and she rested her cheek confidingly against Bridie's shoulder. "I have some that look like angel wings."

"Hush, poppet!" Mistress Carter said. "You should be sleeping." She hastily gathered the tired girl into her arms and carried her back to the bed and then returned to the fire.

Bridie looked at the other woman in silence. The word "angel" hung between them until Bridie reached out impulsively. "Don't you wish for a priest, as I do?"

"Nay, nay," Mistress Carter insisted in a low voice. She did not sit down, but stood hovering near the hearth. "In Scotland we had our faith, but it did not buy bread or pay rents. We knew what we did when we came to Massachusetts for work, and now we are in the Congregation.

This is our home," she said firmly. "Father Dougal knew what we did and blessed us."

"I know, but—" Bridie bit off her words. She knew without being told that she made the woman uneasy, for Bridie was one of few who knew of the family's Catholicism. Willing or reluctant, the Carters were putting their faith behind them and making themselves new.

But that was what Bridie could not manage to do, and Mistress Carter seemed to sense it and to fear it. Sadly, Bridie stood up.

"I won't let on that you are—were—Catholic," she said.

The woman's face went a dull red in the light. "Understand me, Bridie," she whispered, glancing back to where Margaret lay. "I do wish you well, but I have no wish to make trouble, nor stand out from the others. My daughter—"

"I know." Bridie went to the door and knew she would never find what she had looked for from Mistress Carter, but she couldn't blame her. "Good-bye. I won't come again."

Now Bridie felt her homesickness more keenly than ever, and she wandered with no thought to where she went.

Then, up ahead, she heard a door closing. By instinct, she stepped into the shadow again. She did not wish to be seen. Footsteps retreated, and the place was quiet again. She saw she'd walked by the Handy ordinary.

It was quiet, unlike her parents' place. Lights shone fitfully from within as people passed from time to time before the fire. But there was no sound. The place had withal a furtive, unfriendly air, as though the people there had necessary bad business to attend to.

At least her own family did well and prospered at their trade, Bridie thought with relief. It must be a drab, gloomy home for Will, and she softened toward him, placing the blame for his stiff uprightness on the coldness of his house, the sharp, scraping spite of his mother.

The door creaked open, and there Will was, silhouetted against the dim light within. Startled at his sudden appearance even as she thought of him, Bridie let out a cry.

"Who is it?" Will asked, walking toward her.

Bridie backed up, remembering her sharp words at their last meeting. " 'Tis only Bridget MacKenzie," she said. "I haven't come to pinch again," she added when he was silent.

"What do you do out here?"

Will's voice was tired, and Bridie felt a rush of sympathy, imagining the life he led in that cold house. Hers was not the only sadness in Marblehead. "I—I went out to visit a friend," she said.

"A friend?" He sounded distant and somewhat puzzled by the word. He took a few slow steps down the path that ran by the side of his house.

Bridie's heart ached as she fell into step beside him. "Don't you have any friend yourself?" she asked softly. Their footsteps whispered in the night, and the soft air sighed along with them. Bridie saw Will's profile against the stars, saw him tip his head back and gaze upward.

"No, I've no friend," he answered at last.

"Will—" Bridie put her hand on his arm, then withdrew it. "I would be your friend."

Will turned to face her in the darkness, and Bridie felt a strong pull, like the tide, urging her toward him. They stood very close, not speaking, as the ocean's breath fanned their cheeks.

"Bridget, I can't—"

Behind them, the door creaked open again. "I need you, Will," a sharp, cold voice came.

" 'Tis my mother," Will said near Bridie's ear. "Go, she'll be very angry."

"But why should—" Bridie began.

He shook his head and hurried back to the door. Hurt and disappointed, Bridie began to walk away. But she glanced back once. In the narrow gap of the door, Goody Handy stood watching her.

Bridie's hand went up, wanting to sign the cross, but caution stopped her, and she dropped her hand to her side. Shivering again, she hurried home, her long skirt billowing like a wind-filled sail.

Chapter Eight

Bridie arose the following day with a new determination to make her way smooth. She had vowed to Sarah that she would adapt herself, and adapt she would. The Carters could do it, and she had every good reason to try hard, for she loved her family and would not see them hurt. She crossed Front Street and let herself into the shell-strewn yard of the Furness house, where Sarah was sitting.

"I've an idea," she said.

Sarah was letting the hem of a dress down, using the strong sunlight to see her stitches. "Well," she said, not looking up. "Tell me it."

"Goody Handy seems very much set against me," Bridie said. "She has no reason for it, but if as it seems the woman is weak in the head, I can let it pass me by. I will do something to make her know I mean her no harm."

Sarah raised her head and squinted to thread her

needle. She cocked one eye at Bridie. "The work would go wasting," she said dryly.

"I've a special reason for wishing to try, even so," Bridie said, looking away.

Her friend grinned. "Will Handy." She stabbed her needle into the fawn-colored cloth spread across her lap and took two stitches while shaking her head. "You're a brave one. I hope you deem the prize worth the price."

Bridie bent down and took Sarah by the wrists. "I do," she said, smiling. "The faint of heart never win aught worth more than a shilling. Will may be difficult, but he's also good, and I like him."

"So." Sarah looked searchingly at Bridie. "I believe you can do it if it can be done at all."

"We shall see," Bridie replied.

"But I do bid you beware. The woman quizzes her son daily, and he cannot refuse to answer. What you say to him will reach her, of that I'm certain." Sarah pressed her lips together and squinted up at Bridie again. "So if you do like him, watch what you say to him."

Bridie did not take her friend's words to heart. They were too dire, and she was too confident. She only smiled and turned to return to her own house. Bridie had little hope that Goody Handy would take any service from her, but a generous gift might blunt the widow's sharpness.

In one of the cupboards was a store of cordials put up in seasons gone by and used in sparing drops to give sweet flavor to some drinks. Cherry, black currant, and floral elixirs filled small glass flasks with jeweled light.

Bridie took one, and without asking herself if her course was truly a wise one, she ran from the house.

As she burst into the sunny street, a small clutch of women stumbled out of her way in surprise, scattering some chickens as they did.

"I pray pardon, good women," Bridie said, then saw Goody Handy among them. "Lady, I have something I wish to give you."

Will's mother stepped backward, drawing her skirts back also. "I've told you to stay away."

Bridie bade herself remain mild and pleasant. "I thought you might wish a bottle of cordial for the guests at your ordinary," she said firmly, holding out the vial.

"I wish for no such thing." Goody Handy's eyes widened with alarm. "Keep it from me!"

"Good women—" Bridie appealed to the others even as her heart began to race with frustration and hurt. Passersby had stopped in the street, and Goody Furness was watching from her doorway. "My mother made this. It's very good."

"Why give it her, then?" Goody Cooper asked suspiciously.

"Only as an act of friendship," Bridie insisted. She saw her effort flying away into pieces, her goodwill running into the ground like spilled water. With growing distress, she uncorked the bottle. "You have only to smell it to know it is good."

In her eagerness to make Will's mother like her, Bridie stepped toward Goody Handy, her hand outstretched. She tripped over a hen. The vial of cordial flew out of her grasp and spilled half its contents on Goody Handy.

There was a shocked silence from the women, and the stepped-on chicken clucked angrily away. Bridie stood frozen, her hope vanished, and watched the widow staring down at the spreading red stain on her apron.

Then, to everyone's horror, Goody Handy began to cough, her breath coming in gasps. "What has she done to me?" she wheezed, clutching at a companion's sleeve. "Take me away from her."

" 'Tis only a cherry cordial," Bridie whispered. "God's truth, I swear it."

The women surrounding Goody Handy helped her away, and Bridie was left alone. Across the street, Sarah's mother stepped backward into the house and shut the door.

Like one in a dream, Bridie bent down to retrieve the half-empty bottle where it lay in a blood-red stain in the dust.

For several days, Bridie hardly dared raise her eyes to see how people regarded her. Now more than ever, she dared not walk out of step with the folk of Marblehead. She gave up searching the landscape for medicinal plants, for to wander alone might raise eyebrows yet again. She ceased rambling about and confined herself to the village, where the port itself became her new haunt.

On the Sabbath she went humbly with her family to the meeting house and sat with bowed head as the others did, wondering if she only imagined whispering voices behind her. As she left, she saw Goody Handy stare at her, then speak into the Reverend Stoughton's ear. Bridie felt her heart sink. She had truly made an enemy of Will's mother, and perhaps even made an enemy of many others in Marblehead. There was no doubt that there was a coldness in their greetings to her and her family.

And the more Bridie kept her own nature reined in, the more depressed of spirit she became. Only at the harbor, in the company of the wide, inhuman ocean, did her tired soul find some ease. She left for there one morning in spite of the chores she had to do and encountered Goodwife Furness and Sarah in Front Street as she stepped out of the ordinary.

"Good day, Goody Furness," Bridie said. She glanced at Sarah.

"Good day, Bridget," Goody Furness replied stiffly.

"Bridie, will you come to—" Sarah began, but her mother broke in.

"Come, Sarah. We've much to do."

Bridie stood looking down at the trodden earth as Sarah and her mother hurried away down the street.

"Good day, Bridget," said Goody Cooper, passing by with Mistress Carter. Mistress Carter avoided Bridie's eyes and made a fuss of checking in her basket.

Bridie greeted them quietly as she made her way along Front Street. She need not be careful not to smile too wide nor to step too lightly, for her cares hung like a sodden cape from her shoulders and she had no cause for mirth. That Sarah's mother would frown on their friendship now seemed only part of the rest.

When she gained the docks, a boat came in and began unloading its cargo of glistening fish. With listless attention Bridie looked at the bleak dead eye of a massive cod thrown up near her feet. Her great hopes for Massachusetts seemed as blighted to her as that dead fish. She who'd once been so careless and light of heart felt only the heaviness and woe of a hard future trudging ahead of her. All seemed gray and loveless without the liberty to pray as she wished to, or to heal as she knew she could, or to make friends as she might. Her exile was tight and pinching and cold. She remembered Kit's joy for her and Father Dougal's blessing and felt sick.

Numb, Bridie covered her eyes with one hand. She listened to her own slow breathing, to the suck and pull of the waves around the pilings, to the creak and strain of hawsers, the sighing wind, and the keening gulls. She wished she might lie down where she was and not think anymore.

"Mistress MacKenzie?"

She slowly raised her eyes. Will was passing but had stopped. He looked at her with some concern, and his voice was low and gentle. As though against his wishes, he took two hesitant steps toward her and stopped.

Bridie felt a slow revolution somewhere deep inside her and knew that she might begin to cry if she listened to his voice.

"I only look to see how the catch is today," she said tonelessly, turning her face away. With an effort, she forced herself to stand taller and began to walk back the way she'd come. She wanted no reminder of how light she once had been, how she'd tried to win Will's favor and gained nothing but suspicion.

She heard his footsteps on the wooden dock as he approached her, and his voice when he spoke to her was painfully tender. "Bridget—"

"Nay, don't," she protested, turning her back again as he tried to face her. She fought hard to keep the tears from spilling forth, but she could not.

"Let me walk with you." He took her arm to steer her around some pigs and led her away.

For some time, Bridie allowed herself to be directed by him and was glad only to let herself drift along by his side. At last they stopped at the summit, at the burial ground, and Bridie raised her eyes to look out. It was a clear, cool day, and the view went on to the gray horizon, limitless and open. In this place she could stand in the wind forever, until nothing was left of her but the bent grasses where her footsteps had been.

But then Will moved beside her, and she looked up into his face. Behind him was the sky and the radiant, sea-mirrored light of the sun. The calls of the gulls came faintly on the wind, and the salt smell of the ocean mingled with the grass under their feet. His expression was so tender that Bridie did not know what to say.

"You seem different," Will said at last. "What has changed you?"

Bridie spread her hands out before her, gazed at

them, and then let them fall to her side. "My heart—my heart—I'm so sad."

He nodded and drew a deep breath, gesturing with one hand toward the north and west.

"That is Salem that way," he said, one foot up on a red rock. "It was used to be called Naumkeag for the savages that lived there, but that name was changed. I was born there and only came here last autumn. Two years since, my father shipped on the *Charity* that was lost at sea, and my mother went nearly demented with the loss of him. And so we came here to try over."

Bridie looked up at him and saw that he felt a stranger here too. His manner was changed, as hers was, and once again she saw the warm, kind young man behind the dignified front. He was as lonely as she. Although he did not say so with words, still he was offering an apology for his mother's bitterness and suspicion, was ready to befriend her in spite of everything. The breeze played through his hair, blowing it back from his forehead and making him squint as he spoke. Bridie was shocked to realize she wished he might take her hand.

Blushing, she drove such thoughts from her head.

"Does your mother's trade do well?" she asked, bidding herself not remember the warmth of his hand on her elbow as he'd led her to this lookout.

"Not well, no. I would have it otherwise," Will said with a frown. "If my father had not died, I might have gone to Harvard College to be a minister, for my mother has property of her own. But now she cannot bear for me to be away from her, so I stay and help as I can."

Bridie walked a few paces, feeling the breeze on her cheek. "Yet she does not seem happy in her trade, even with you always by her."

"I fear she has not the heart it needs," Will said. "Those who look for smiles and pleasant words go elsewhere." He looked pointedly at her and smiled.

Bridie took the compliment shyly and stole a glance at him from beneath her lashes. She marveled that a Puritan such as he could show such gentleness and charm. His smile transformed his face, making him beautiful, and Bridie found she must look away.

"I found a nest of robin hatchlings up here. Will you see it?" Will asked her.

Bridie felt suddenly uplifted, and she could not but smile back at him. The morbid fancies that had overtaken her were scattered by the wind and sun, and by Will's gesture of friendship. "Thank you, I will."

His smile lingered for another moment, and then he took a step backward. " 'Tis only over here."

Moment by moment, his upright manner dissolved into a lighter, more boyish one. He hurried, almost running, to a crab tree nearby. Bridie wanted to warn him he'd frighten the birdlings if he was too loud and fast, but she also did not want to make him slow down. She ran to catch up.

"They're here," Will said, standing with his head among the leaves. He held out his hand to beckon, and Bridie followed him into a bower. "Just there."

Bridie stood on tiptoes, all too aware of the green closeness that hid them from the rest of the world. The nest was just above her, and she heard the faint, delicate cheeping of the birds. "I—I canna see into it," she whispered.

Will looked at her, and then at the nest, and a blush colored his face as their eyes met again in silence. Bridie knew he'd have to lift her if she was to see it, and she backed up, her heart racing. "I wouldn't want to disturb them," she said breathlessly.

"No. They won't fear you," Will replied, his voice rough. "Come."

He put his hands to her waist, but did not try to lift her. Bridie looked up at him and thought she might cry again from the strength of the emotion that held her. Their green bower was still and close and quiet, and nothing else was or would be except them. Will gazed into her eyes.

"Bridie," he whispered. "What have you done to me?"

She shook her head, unable to speak. She could feel the warmth of his hands pressing against her through her dress, and she raised her own hands to his chest to push him away. But she did not push.

"You're so beautiful," Will said. "I think you have bewitched me."

Bridie broke suddenly away and ducked to pass beneath the low branches into the sunlight again. Her pulse beat loudly in her ears. She held on to a branch to steady herself in the strong light.

Will followed her out. "I didn't mean—"

"No." Bridie cut him off with a sharp movement of

her hand. Then she drew a deep breath and brought forth a smile. "Thank you for showing me the nest."

Will cleared his throat, his solemn front restored. "I'll say good day to you, then."

In silence, Bridie watched him as he made his way down the steep hill, striding purposefully back toward town. Her knees suddenly buckled, and she had to sit down at once on the grass. Then she looked out at the ocean and smiled, her cheeks aglow. She stayed there for long minutes, letting her strength grow within her again, and stealing a glance now and then at the crab tree.

"Will Handy," she whispered. When she could trust herself to stand steadily, she rose and set out for home. She hummed as she picked her way down the hill.

" 'And rattlin' roarin' Willie, ye're welcome home to me.' "

With a longer step and lighter spirit, Bridie went into the town and made her way up Front Street. As she opened the door of the ordinary, she cocked her ear for the sounds of her family within. But all was silent, and she was surprised to see no one in the place.

"Mother? Johnny?"

A quick survey of the garden told her none of her family was there, so she hurried back inside and climbed up the ladderlike stairs. There were voices above.

"What is it?" Bridie asked, squeezing into the crowded room she shared with her brother.

On the bed, John lay shuddering and wrapped in blankets while their parents bent over him.

"What is it?" Bridie asked again, flying to the bed and

leaning over her brother. John looked up at her, shivering, but said nothing.

"The lad took a dunking," Master MacKenzie said. He walked to the window and looked out, ill at ease. "But he didn't come home to change into dry clothing. He's been taking a chill all the day long, and now has taken a fever on him."

"Och, now, my bonny." Bridie collected her skirts so she could sit beside John on the bed. Tenderly she placed one hand on his brow and was shocked at the high heat of him.

"He'll soon be right," Mistress MacKenzie declared with a smile at her boy. It was a cosseting, coaxing, cozying smile, the one given to frightened children to sweep away their fears like a brisk broom. "We'll keep him warm, and he has a pan of coals at his feet."

"Aye," the father echoed, turning away from staring out the window. "He'll soon be right."

Bridie sent a swift look to her parents. The case was more serious than her mother let on, but Bridie did not make any comment. Instead she tucked Johnny well in and swept back his hair.

"I'll make him a hot drink," she said, beginning to rise.

Master MacKenzie stumbled in his hurry to be out of Bridie's way, and then, with a frightened look at John, left the room. Bridie could hear his clattering haste down the ladder and his swift footsteps across the floor of the room below. The door of the house banged open and shut. Surprised, Bridie looked up at her mother with a questioning glance.

The woman beckoned with a nod of her head, and led Bridie out of John's hearing.

"Your father takes it hard when Johnny sickens," she said softly. "We had another boy here, you know."

Bridie felt the heart drop out of her. "No, Mother, I did not know it."

"Aye. We called him Charlie." Mistress MacKenzie gripped her elbows with work-rough hands and furrowed her brow as though looking into the past. "He died of a fever when he was a babe, before we even could send word of his birth to you and your grandfather."

"Mother—"

"Now, sit with your brother," Bridie's mother commanded, pushing her to the bed.

Bridie made as if to leave. "I should make a posset for him or a hot drink."

John whimpered and made a grab for her hand. "Stay, Bridie."

"Stay with him," Mistress MacKenzie pleaded. She met Bridie's eyes and nodded urgently. The little boy twined his hot fingers around Bridie's, and she relented. She was truly alarmed at how hot he was and how red and dry his skin, as though he'd been tossed in the fire to toast.

"Aye, darling, aye. I'll stay with you." She leaned back against the headboard and pulled him into her arms. He curled his trembling body against her trustfully, fragile as a bird.

"I'll heat some cider," their mother said.

Mistress MacKenzie left the room, and Bridie rocked her brother gently. "Poor foolish boy," she scolded in a soft voice. "What did you think you were doing? The wind off the water is treacherous."

"The birds were many," John said through chattering teeth. He pressed his cheek against her. "I couldn't leave the flakes."

"Devil take the cod." Bridie looked down, smoothing back the hair from his brow. He should sweat, but did not. It was early yet, though, and no harm might come to him. If the fever broke in a few hours, she'd know he was mending.

And if it did not break, she had herbs still to help him along. No notion of "God's will be done" darkened her thoughts. She had the skill to help her brother, and she'd sooner die herself than forsake him.

"Lie still, darling," she said, easing herself out from under his small weight. She laid him back on the bed and began searching through the packets of medicine she'd brought with her. The wormwood she wanted was no-where to be found, though, and for some moments she sat in wondering distress.

Then she remembered Margaret Carter and shook her head. She'd used up her physics for fever on board the *Rose,* and had none left.

"Don't fash yourself, bonny boy," she whispered as her brother made a small fitful sound behind her. She lightly brushed his hot cheek with her fingers, then slipped out of the room as her mother returned.

111

"Where are you going?" Mistress MacKenzie asked in an undertone. She held a steaming mug in her hand.

"I'll be back when I've something to help Johnny with," Bridie said, not meeting her mother's look.

At the head of the ladder, Bridie paused for the space of a heartbeat. She dreaded hearing her mother call her back, warn her off. She did not know what she might say if she found that her mother felt as so many others did.

But Mistress MacKenzie said nothing at all, either of warning or encouragement. Bridie let out her breath, and then climbed down. As she entered the main gathering room, a group of men came in from outdoors.

"Good day to you—" began one in a hearty voice.

Shaking her head, Bridie pushed by them. She did not look to see if they stared at her for her odd behavior. She cared little for their raised eyebrows now.

In the garden, she bent over the burgeoning plants, here rubbing a leaf between her fingers, there breaking off a flower head and tasting the petals with gingerly care. Yet with all the living green around her, there were none of the herbal cures she trusted well. Too many of the simples for which she knew recipes required seeds or herbage dried to increase its potency. Here in late May there were no seeds, and the pale green flush of first growth was too young to yield her anything. Frowning in concentration, she let herself out through the gate and walked slowly up the beaten-earth street.

She kept her gaze trained down to the ground, scanning the edges of the paths, the manure heaps, the rocky swales, and the meadows of grass as she went farther and farther from home. She kept hoping for a glimpse of something useful, something she would recognize without fear that it was something different from what she knew. She wanted tormentil, knighten milfoil, coltsfoot, or any of the many other plants that could bring on the sweat of fever and help to clear the lungs. If John was to develop an inflammation of the chest, she must be prepared for coughing, pain, and chills. All that she knew of herbs and plants crowded in her imagination, calling out names and preparations, urging her to beware of the poisonous misuse of potent properties. She was deaf and blind to everything but the plants around her. She knew she must get back to John.

With a cry, she bent down and plucked up a fine-toothed, delicate frond of yarrow. She bruised it roughly between her fingers, smelled it, and licked the green stain. It was the same yarrow that she knew and would help her brother. Quickly she dropped to her knees and pulled handfuls of the herbs, drawing up what plants she could see in the failing light. When her hands were full, she raced back home, stumbling on rocks in her haste and fiercely dragging her skirt away from the grasping brambles.

With eyes bright and cheeks flushed, Bridie swept into the ordinary, bringing with her a swirl of salt air and green scents. Her hair was tumbled in disarray about her shoulders, and she breathed hard from running. At the fire, a group of men gaped at her in surprise over their tankards, halted their talk, and nodded cautious greetings. The crackling of resin in the fire snapped through the silence. Her father sat staring into the hearth and did not look up.

Bridie caught her breath, trying to form words.

"Good evening to you, sirs," she whispered, judging her own strange appearance from their startled faces. Then she looked down, following the gaze of Master Carter, and saw that many of them noted her hands. She held great bunches of yarrow torn up by the roots. Clumps of dirt sifted onto the wooden floor with a soft patter. There was no mistaking the wildness and frenzy with which she'd plucked the plants, and, too late, she drew her hands behind her back.

She felt the color burn in her cheeks and tried to think of a way to explain it. She must appear a madwoman to them.

But a footstep up above drove all thought of that from her mind. Only catching her breath on a gasp, Bridie turned and ran from the room.

"I've something that might help," she exclaimed as she gained the top floor.

Her mother sat by the bed, washing John's face and hands with a wet cloth. "Shh," she murmured, wringing out the cloth.

"Does he sweat?" Bridie asked.

Her mother shook her head. John's eyes were closed, but he whimpered in his sleep. His hands twitched from time to time as though he had a pain that he could not reach. Mistress MacKenzie looked at Bridie and at the dirty wreckage of leaves in her hands. "What have you?" she asked in a bewildered voice.

114

"Yarrow," Bridie said, placing it all on the top of an oaken barrel. She began stripping the stems, and the barrel top was soon covered with a delicate tracery like green lace.

"It may not work, being so fresh," Bridie said. "But a tea may bring on sweating, and that's what Johnny is needing now."

There was a hoarse, harsh, honking cough from the boy, like the bark of a seal. " 'Tis already in his lungs," Mistress MacKenzie murmured, washing his hands again with cool water.

Bridie stood in a fog for a moment, gazing blankly at the little boy. He was worsening fast. "Och, my dearie," she whispered.

Her mother glanced her way, and Bridie realized that her own hands were clasped as though in prayer. Yanking them apart, Bridie turned back to her work. It was time to see if the folk of Marblehead were right in their suspicion of her, to see if she could change what they saw as God's will and make her brother well. For herself, she did not believe God wanted John dead: He had given her the skill to heal, and she would use it or be damned.

Long into the night, Bridie and her mother sat up with John. His fever grew worse, and his skin was so hot to touch that it made Bridie shudder each time she pressed her cheek to his. Against his pitiful cries, she forced the yarrow tea between his lips, tenderly wiped away what he could not swallow, and forced again. The light of one tallow candle licked across the rough walls, touching on nail head and knothole, the fringe of a blanket, John's small wooden cup, the wooden poppet clutched in his hand. The flame swayed and dipped in the draft, lighting some things to life one moment and dropping them into darkness the next. Bridie went and stood before the candle, holding her hand in front of the flame so that the edges of her fingers glowed red.

"He must sweat soon," her mother said behind her. "He must, or he'll rave and become wild in the head from the heat of it—"

Mistress MacKenzie stopped speaking when her voice cracked. Bridie felt the pain in her mother's heart touch her own, and knew that both were thinking of little Charlie long buried. She spread her fingers, letting the light of the candle pour between them. Her eyes were dazzled, and the rest of the room fell suddenly back into darkness around her, and she was frightened. The window was ahead of her, but she could see nothing through it.

"This is a hard place to live, Mother," Bridie said, staring blindly at the black, blank glass. "It's an unco hard place. I cannot wonder now that you left me behind when you came."

Mistress MacKenzie let go her breath in a long sigh. "Did we right in bringing you now?"

Bridie felt her throat swell with tears. "I do believe so."

Bridie stood as she was for another moment, but she feared she would cry with the great fear that had closed in so quickly around her. Without turning to say a word to her mother, she slipped out of the room and climbed down the ladder.

Outside, the moon shone on Marblehead and cast it all in ghostly pale light. The silence was as deep as the ocean, so deep that Bridie could hear the ocean itself: the whispering lap of waves on the shingle, the rippling curl that ran over the tops of the waves, and the muffled breath of the tide as it rose. Bridie walked a few paces into the darkness, letting her mind drift on the soft sounds.

She was not frightened outdoors as she had been at her mother's side. She knew she had come to a hard place, but she knew that all places were hard. She would risk anything to make her brother's way easier. If the yarrow did not work, she would try something else. She would try until he died or until he became well again.

But for the moment, she tarried outside, reveling in the nameless drift of the night. Only at such a time was Bridie out of the eye of Marblehead. Only at such a time could she feel that she knew who she was. She knew she was a person to gainsay the rules if the rules were wrong, and she'd take what came of it to help John.

With such a bleak resolution, she put her hands together and bowed her head, speaking inside as she had never done, making vows, opening her soul. *Save Johnny, save Johnny,* she prayed over and over. *Save my brother.*

When she turned, she saw the faint glow of the candle in the window of her room, and she went back inside.

Chapter Nine

By MORNING, Bridie was close to distraction with worry and sleeplessness. She had dozed fitfully during the night with John's head in her lap. But she had hovered near the brink of waking at all times, always alert to her brother's feverish tossing. And each time she waked, she recalled Will holding her under the tree as she held John, and the shadows in her heart would be brightened. Now her arms ached from keeping them around John, but she would not move to disturb him. She laid her head back and stared at the window as it turned from black to gray to hazy white, and at last to palest blue.

"How is he?" Mistress MacKenzie asked, coming awake in her chair by the bed. She leaned close and felt John's brow.

"No different, I fear." Bridie looked down at the helpless child in her arms and felt a wave of panic. She had ministered to him all night to no avail. "I have not helped at all," she added in despair.

Her mother shook her head. "If God wills it to—"

"Don't say such things!" Bridie exclaimed in a hoarse whisper. "How can you say it? Can you be such a Puritan?"

Mistress MacKenzie looked away, her throat working as she tried to swallow. Tears glinted at the corners of her eyes.

"Bridie, God's plan for Massachusetts is suffering and want, or so we must assume, for that is all we ever see here. He sends down the French and the Indian to plague our boats, ice and rain to choke us, and sickness to kill our children. Who are *you* to say it should not be so?"

Too shocked and angry to speak, Bridie laid her brother gently down and left the room to go downstairs. Fear and anger and doubt ran riot through her, fear that her mother was giving up, anger that her father only shied away from the sickroom, and doubt that she herself could do anything for her brother except watch him slip down and away forever, like a shell through the water.

She did not know enough of the local plants. She was as useless as anyone who knew nothing of the properties of herbs at all. Pacing, clenching her hands together, she strode back and forth before the dead fire in the gathering room. She would not let the God of Massachusetts have John if she could help it.

"I'm going out," she said as her father came dazedly in.

"Where to?"

"To find a sagamore," Bridie said with defiance.

119

Master MacKenzie's face paled. "You must not go to the Indians, Daughter. They're heathen and our enemies."

"Which is what everyone believes *me* to be!" Bridie retorted as she opened the door. "I know full well Goody Handy and others think I tried to poison her, and I cannot clear my name with them anymore. But I'll not sit in the meeting house while my brother dies."

She stepped outside into the path of two women. That they'd heard her there was no doubt. They looked at Bridie askance and pulled away.

Biting back a bitter oath, Bridie turned and headed for the edge of town with no thought but finding one of the Indians and seeing if indeed they knew herbal lore as well. The close-built houses seemed to press in around her, crowding the streets and staring at her with a judging air, and Bridie walked faster and faster, putting a stitch in her side. But the tears came faster and blinded her, and she had to stop.

"Help me, Saint Mary," she whispered, covering her face with both hands. "Help me."

When she took away her hands, it was to see Will walking toward her. He noticed her at the same time and smiled and quickened his pace. Bridie stood, weeping silently, until he stood before her.

"Will," Bridie said, looking up at him and wiping away her tears. "Will, my brother is very ill."

His smile faded, and he faded once again into the stiff and dignified Puritan she'd first met. He drew a breath, as though for a lengthy sermon. "Bridget—"

"Don't you speak to me of God's will," Bridie cut in impetuously. "I will not hear it."

"I wasn't."

She pushed by him, wishing she had not stopped and looked to him for help. She had known from the start what his beliefs were. Only weakness had made her wish he would support her.

"Stay—can I help you?" Will asked, running to fall into step by her side.

Bridie shook her head, but could not send him away.

"I am taking the ferry to Salem. Can I get you anything?" Will tried again in the earnest, solemn manner that had once made Bridie yearn to tickle his ears with a feather.

Now it only sent an ache of longing through her. She wanted his friendship more than ever.

"Let me help you," Will pleaded. His eyes were bluer than the horizon as he looked down at her, urging her to place her trust in him.

Bridie felt she was falling forward, falling into the blue. She swayed for a moment. Will caught her arm to steady her, and she sensed she had crossed over some line. She could not hold back from him.

"I'm going to seek out one of the sagamores," she whispered, though every grain of caution in her warned her not to admit it to him.

"A savage?" Will asked in dismay. "They're of the Devil."

"I don't believe that," Bridie insisted. "But if they are, I don't care. If they can help me cure John, the Devil is not so bad. Do you know where they are? Will you take me to them?"

Will looked even more shocked, and his face flushed as he glanced quickly around.

"Will you help me find them? You say you would help me, so do!" Bridie's voice rose in a frightened wail.

When he did not answer her, she felt a flood of disappointment so powerful that she thought it would knock her down and sweep her under. She drew a choking breath and walked quickly away, stumbling on the uneven path. Inside she felt hollow and cold, as though the wind were blowing through her, and her greatest fear was that it would blow her clean away.

Then she heard Will's footsteps catching up to her, and he kept his place by her side. Too overwrought to speak, Bridie stole a look at him. His expression was grim, and she knew he disapproved strongly of what she did. But he was there. She cared about nothing else.

They did not speak as Will led the way along a well-worn footpath. It snaked its way inland, past the great freshwater ponds and the roving flocks of sheep and kine. The sky overhead was a vivid blue, and away from the shore the breeze was stilled. The air grew warm and close, with a humming of bees. A rabbit burst out from under Bridie's feet and dashed ahead, dodging first right and then left in its panic to flee. Will's pace lengthened. His face was set and stern.

And so Bridie had nearly to run to keep up with him as he strode ahead on long legs. The sleepless night and worry dragged at her feet, and the warm, humid air was hard to breathe. To one side, the trees formed a dark, fathomless barrier. Bridie felt the close air press in on her, and the fancy grew in her that eyes were watching from the black cover of the wood. With every faltering step she glanced toward that cover, knowing how dreadful it would be to be lost in woods that went on forever. She might be lost, might wander, and John would die.

She stopped, gulping for air, as the edges of her vision clouded over. Will was several paces ahead. Bridie tried to call out to him, but the droning of the bees filled her ears and she could not speak, and then she fell forward onto her knees.

It seemed only a moment later that she opened her eyes, but Will was kneeling by her side and holding her against him. Faintly, she sensed his heart beating against her ear. She closed her eyes again, resting within his arms.

"You've swooned, Bridie," he said. "Forget this folly. Let me take you home."

At first, Bridie could not think what folly he meant, could not think where she was going. But then she remembered her brother, and she struggled to rise. "No, I must find the sagamore," she gasped, swaying again.

"Bridie, no!" Will pulled her back down to the ground and pressed his hands to her shoulders.

Too weak to fight, Bridie slumped and put her head to her knees, weeping into her apron. "He'll die, he'll die if I can't get him something to break the fever," she sobbed, shaking her head from side to side. "Help me or leave me, but don't make me go back."

"You're a bold, willful, stubborn girl," Will burst out angrily.

"Aye. I am willful and stubborn when it's someone I love." Bridie raised her face and looked at him for a long moment. "Will you or nill you help me?"

Will clenched his jaw and looked away toward the shadowy, ungoverned woods. That he was out of his element and awkward with it was clear. Every line in his face proclaimed him as an adversary to nature, and even to Bridie, who knew how to walk in step with it. He struggled visibly to nod in assent.

"I will," he said heavily. He held out his hand to her to help her up, but did not smile or look at her directly.

Bridie left her hand in his, grateful that for once she was not the subject of curious eyes. But he had not slackened his pace, in fact walked faster than ever.

"You need not go farther than you must," Bridie told him. "When we're near, only tell me where to go and you may leave me. I know you have no wish to traffic with the Indians."

Will nodded. The path curved around a hill, and then there was a wide field of corn and the Indian encampment.

Bridie stopped short in surprise. Coming on it so abruptly brought a rush of fear and uncertainty down upon her. Without reckoning in full, she had run headlong for help. But now she was afraid. For all she knew, the people here were indeed wicked and dangerous. She crossed herself, not caring if Will saw.

Then she looked warily about her. The houses of the

Indians were long, built of logs and mud. Each was framed with bent saplings and covered with sheets of bark. No men were evident, but women and girls worked over fires, and scraped hides. Dogs and children ran yelling between them. One little boy was naked in the heat, and Bridie turned her face away, mortified.

"Here they are," Will said harshly, dropping her hand.

He looked around him in disgust. His nostrils appeared pinched, his blue eyes clouded with loathing.

With a pounding heart, Bridie walked forward, waiting to be noticed. She fixed her gaze on a young woman pounding corn in a wooden mortar and walked steadily on, not daring to stop or look about. At last the woman looked up, and all around the other women stopped their work as one by one they saw Bridie in their midst.

"I need medicines," Bridie said. Her voice croaked hoarsely, and she cleared her throat. "Do you have medicines for fever?"

Women crowded around her, staring. The strangeness of their faces, their braided, oiled hair, their clothes, wrapped Bridie in a fog of near panic. She searched the crowd for the girl she had concentrated on at first and repeated her question in a rising, fearful voice.

"Do you have medicines for fever?" she asked. She did not even know if they spoke her language. An ungovernable cry of fear and grief tried to make its way up through Bridie, and she fought it. She must know if they would help her. She had no other hope.

"It is for a child," she added.

"Your child?"

One of the older women came forward and looked frankly at Bridie's body. Bridie felt her face flush scarlet and shook her head. "No, my brother. I knew some plants, some medicines where I came from. But I do not know the plants that grow here. Can you help me?"

"Yes. Come."

Bridie felt herself being led by the elbows, in the midst of the group of women, to the nearest dwelling. Wide-eyed, her heart racing, she looked back over her shoulder. Will stood where she had left him, staring at her.

He had brought her this far against his judgment, but he could go no farther. To help her brother, Bridie had to submit herself to these women, savage or no, heathen or no, enemy or no. She ducked her head and followed them inside.

A noisy babble of voices met her as she entered, and her eyes failed her in the sudden darkness. All was new and strange, and Bridie could scarcely take in what she saw as she slowly regained her sight. The lodgepoles were hung with finely woven baskets, tools, and bundles of hides, and along the floor were ranged vessels of all shapes and kinds. The women were sitting on a fur rug, beckoning Bridie over. Still fearful, but curious and hopeful, Bridie gathered her skirts and knelt with them.

"This root is making strong blood," the most senior woman told Bridie as she began opening leather packets. "English call this plant coneflower."

"Coneflower—what does it look like?" Bridie asked.

"You know a flower you are calling daisy?" the woman said, and when Bridie nodded, she held out a mussel shell and rubbed her callused thumb along the smooth, purple inside of the curve. "It is a daisy of this color."

Her voice was low and her accent odd to Bridie's ear. But Bridie felt a great relief and gratitude that the woman spoke English and that she was ready to help. As she watched, more packets were opened and laid out on the floor between them.

"English are calling this boneset. It makes sweating when we are using leaves and stems. It has a very bad taste, and you must be adding honey.

"This is tree bark you are calling wild cherry. It is making a cough."

Bridie listened carefully, memorizing the uses of the plants in infusions and teas, noting the names, searching her memory for their relatives. The women leaned toward her, as though urging her to remember, to learn, to succeed. Bridie felt their encouragement lifting her up and was grateful, although she could not think of a way to thank them. When she had accepted a small grass basket of fine weave, filled with the bark and roots and dried leaves she'd learned, she nodded her gratitude and bowed as she stood up. A small boy of John's age came in and stood shyly behind an upright pole. Bridie smiled at him.

"My brother—" Tears flooded her eyes, and Bridie fought hard to control them. The women looked at her silently, their dark eyes intent on hers.

"My brother is a good boy, like this boy," she whispered.

The child ran to a young woman and buried his head against her side in a fit of bashfulness, and everyone smiled indulgently. Bridie, too full of heart to say anything more, turned and left.

The brightness blinded her for a moment. She did not know if she was in a Naumkeag village or the village of another Indian people. Whoever these people were, though, they were no savages. Bridie looked in amazement at the life around her. She wanted to know them more, and she let her gaze travel over fire and dog and corn until it came to Will.

He stood there at the edge of the field like a black shadow, out of place and somehow ominous. Bridie shivered, remembered the urgency of her mission, and clasped the basket to her. Then she ran to join Will and return to Marblehead.

Chapter Ten

THE WILD CHERRY, the boneset, the coneflower: the Indians' physic pushed John's fever into a sweat readily. From then on, it was a simple matter for Bridie and her mother to keep him comfortable, to feed him ale with honey for strength, and then stamped corn-meal with milk as his appetite slowly grew on him.

Sometime in the second night of Bridie's care for her brother, she heard a crack and then a rumbling crash somewhere not far away.

"What might that have been, I wonder?" Mistress MacKenzie said, standing by the window and cupping her hand to look out at the night. "It had the sound of some building falling to the earth."

Bridie pulled up the covers that John kept pushing away and listened as the voices below grew loud and then quiet again, and the street door opened to admit another burst of sound. Master MacKenzie was serving down below on his own, and trade was brisk.

"Perhaps Goody Bull has finally broken through the floor of her house," Bridie said with a tired smile. "That lady surely is large enough to crack any floor."

"Hush, now," her mother said, laughing. She stood over the bed and looked gravely down at her son for a while.

"Where did you find those medicines?" she asked after a wordless, waiting pause. "How came you to know them?"

Bridie wiped a cloth across her brother's damp brow. Someone below roared with laughter. "Don't ask me, Mother," Bridie said quietly. "It will only pain you to know."

"Oh, lassie, lassie." Bridie's mother shook her head slowly. "What have you done?"

"Saved his life, I believe."

"Yes." Mistress MacKenzie walked away again to the window, and she spoke so softly Bridie thought she was only thinking out loud. "I only hope it won't be as I fear."

"What do you fear?" Bridie asked.

Her mother looked back, smiled sadly, and shrugged. " 'Tis nothing," she said, walking to Bridie and holding her close. "I fear nothing. Get you something to eat, my girl. I can bide here with the boy."

Nodding, Bridie climbed wearily down the ladder to the floor below. In the room next to where her parents slept, the company of men raised a such a din that Bridie felt tired just to hear them. Rather than join the noise and the commotion, she let herself out the back door and walked to and fro in the garden.

The moon was a crescent, rocking on its back over the water, and the warm, moist air that flowed around Bridie brought with it the mingled scents of brine and fish and thyme and the faint sweet smell of trodden cow dung in the road. As she walked, the hem of her skirt brushed against the silvery green stalks of lavender, and that scent, too, rose up to touch her cheeks and curl through her hair.

Sighing, Bridie went to the fence and bent down to feel the rosebush. In the darkness, she could see it with her hands, smell the strong life in it. The two-month-old grafts had taken strongly, and as she brushed her fingers up the slender stems of new leaflets, she felt a flower bud.

"Brave thing," Bridie said, smiling to herself. She closed her eyes. "Brave Johnny. Brave lad."

Across the way, the door of the Furness house opened, and a tall figure stepped into the wan moonlight.

"Bridie? Is it you?"

Bridie stood up, and Sarah came to the fence. "How does your brother?"

"Better now, thank God," Bridie said.

Sarah's eyes reflected the moon as she glanced around. "Did you cure him?"

"I—" Bridie wanted to tell Sarah of her visit to the Indians but thought better of it. The fewer people who knew, the fewer people were at risk for it. "He's a strong boy. I think he cured himself."

"I'm glad." Sarah loitered a moment, seeming as though she would say something further. "I heard Goody Handy speak against you today," she said.

131

Bridie shook her head. "She always speaks against me. But this night I've not the strength to worry over it."

"You might wish to know that Will spoke for you," Sarah whispered.

"Spoke for me?" Bridie asked, her heart rising. "What did he say?"

"His mother called you brazen, but he said brave. He recounts your words and deeds to prove your worth. But I fear he caught an earful for his pains."

Bridie let her breath out slowly, and then inhaled the calming scent of lavender again. He was her friend and her ally, was Will, and all that had happened on the way to the Indians had brought them close. He would defend her, even to his mother. "Thank you for telling me."

"I thought you should know. And Bridie?"

Bridie stiffened at the worried sound in Sarah's voice.

"My mother—she asks me not to consort with you. It is only because she does not know you as I do and listens to idle gossip. But I know you are not bad or brazen—or —or any of the things they say."

"I know what they say," Bridie said with resignation. She reached out and found her friend's hand in the dark. "I will not seek you out if it will hurt your standing here. But I thank you."

Sarah nodded. "Good night," she said, running lightly across the street to her own home.

Feeling somewhat refreshed and heartened again, Bridie let herself out through the wicket gate. Will and Sarah both supported her despite their mothers, and she was glad for it. She went into the ordinary through the front door, where she stepped into the noise and confusion of laughter and argumentation.

"Let me help," she said, joining her father at the cellar hole. He was filling up pitchers of ale from the barrels cooling below.

She took one from him and looked to see who beckoned. Masters Bull and Penworthy raised their tankards to her.

As she poured the foaming ale into Bull's mug, Bridie remembered what she had said about Goody Bull and the crash she'd heard. She almost laughed.

"Sirs," she said, keeping her face demure. "Did you hear a crash and a crack a short time ago? Do you know what it could have been?"

"A crash and a crack, do you say?" Penworthy repeated loudly. When he saw he'd gathered the attention of the men closest by, he winked broadly. "A crash and a crack it was indeed. They say the Devil himself came into town and smote the ground with his hoof so hard that the earth cracked open and swallowed Trelawney into the lower depths."

A roar of laughter filled the room, and Bridie glanced around to see if the butt of this joke was there. Trelawney sat in his usual glowering, truculent aloofness in the corner and scorned to hear the fun.

"Nay, nay," Bull said, casting a stern eye on Penworthy. "I have myself just seen the cause, and it was the shed of Goody Handy's house that came down."

"And if her house goes next, it'll mean all the more trade for our host, MacKenzie." Penworthy laughed.

"And if her house goes next," Trelawney spoke up bitingly with a sly glance at Bridie, "we'll know where to look for the cause of it."

The silence was immediate, and there was a subtle withdrawing from Trelawney by the other men. Yet also there was a withdrawing from Bridie, or so she imagined.

Master MacKenzie banged a pitcher down on the plank table, causing heads to turn and glances to fly to and fro among the company. Bridie's father strode quickly to Trelawney, grabbing the man's soiled collar.

"You've had your fill, Cornishman." Master MacKenzie dragged Trelawney up and pitched him toward the door.

"I have not!" Trelawney spluttered, his eyes popping.

The crowd of men parted as Trelawney stumbled through.

"The tithing man warned me off serving you over-much," Bridie's father said, breathing hard. "I deem you've had your fill, but you may get you to Widow Handy's if you still have a thirst on you. I'll not pour any more of my good brew onto your sneaking, spiteful insinuations."

Bridie stood, stricken, in the middle of the room with the serving jug of ale in her hands. Many of the men looked curiously from her to her father. He still breathed hard and looked defiantly around at the company. The color had flooded to his craggy face, and his eyes shone with the fierceness of a Scots clan chief.

"Any other man who has aught to say of my daughter may say it now," Master MacKenzie declared boldly. "She's a good lass and has saved my son's life this day."

None spoke. Bridie's very eyes felt hot with shame and indignation, for the hints that were in the air. At last Master Bowman cleared his throat.

"I'll have another dram, lass," he said in a loud voice, holding his tankard out to her.

Bridie's hands shook slightly as she lifted the jug, and it clattered against the lip of the pewter tankard.

" 'Twas a goodly thing you did, tending your brother," Bowman said kindly.

Bridie raised her eyes to his face and met his sympathetic glance. Then he smiled and nodded as the conversation bubbled up again around them. "Your family is well liked," he said. "And all know your brother is a good, proper boy."

"I thank you," Bridie whispered, allowing herself a smile. "Thank you."

When she dared to look to the other men, she was glad and relieved to see that they did not shy away from her gaze. They nodded or gave her friendly smiles.

"We're not all such dour folk as it may sometimes seem," Penworthy told her as she filled his tankard. "Some may frown on the arts you know, even some you've helped. But you've saved your brother and that cannot be such a very bad thing."

Bridie thanked him, but inside she was uneasy. She could not judge how kind they would be should they discover where she'd been for her medicines. Turning a blind eye to the Devil and his works was one thing for these superstitious fishing people; turning a blind eye to the Indian was another. None had seen the Devil with his own eyes, but all had seen the Indian and the destruction he'd wrought on the fisheries.

So Bridie would not trouble anyone with the knowledge of what she'd done, and her parents would not willfully bring down trouble by spreading that news abroad. With somewhat stronger confidence, Bridie continued to serve the folk in the ordinary until the tithing man came by and proclaimed it time to close for the night.

Master MacKenzie shut the door behind the last man, and Bridie sat near the fire, looking into the embers.

"Thank you, Father," she said as he sat beside her.

In silence, he took her hand and twined his fingers through hers, staring into the fire also. He looked tired, and the dying flames reflected only dimly in his eyes.

"Well. We shall see what this night brings," he said with a sigh.

Bridie stared at him. "Why? What should it bring?"

"Who may say? Tempers and tides are always on the change. We shall see what this night brings."

Shivering, Bridie clasped her fingers more tightly around his. "I did not know peace would be so hard to find here. I did not look to fight so hard."

"Aye, lass. This is Massachusetts. Fighting hard is what we do."

Bridie looked out on the next morning with some trepidation, for she feared that indeed her secret would be let out. None knew where she had gone but her father and Will, and neither would betray her. Of her father's silence she was sure. As for Will, she was certain that the unspoken feelings that had passed between them bound them. She stood by the window, her eyes trained on the distant line of the Neck across the harbor, and absently turned her old wooden poppet over and over in her hands. She missed Will's solemn company.

"Bridie?" came John's voice.

"Laddie!" She crossed the room swiftly.

John made a feeble effort to sit up, but Bridie kept him back. "I'm hungry," he said, still struggling to raise himself.

"Hungry, is it? And should I fetch and carry and feed you pottage like a wee babe?" Bridie teased.

"I'm no babe," John said. His cheeks were pale, and he looked small and wan lying in the bed. Bridie had to smile at his spirit.

"Of course you're not. You're the king of England and I'm happy to do your bidding. You bide a wee while and I'll be back with summat tasty to tempt you with."

She busied herself downstairs, mixing cornmeal and honey and milk and heating it over the fire. Her mother opened the doors and windows, and began sweeping the large room with a withy broom. Bridie told her how well John did that morning, and added the last of the coneflower to the steaming bowl of samp before she carried it upstairs.

"Now, my royal princeling," she sang out. "This is a fine gruel fit for a king, all mixtie-maxtie with honey and good things." She made herself comfortable on the bed

137

beside her brother, rested the bowl in her lap, and fed him and herself in turn with the same spoon.

"Bridie," John said, licking his lips. The color was already seeping back into his cheeks, and he sat up against the headboard unaided. "I want to show you a place I know."

"And what place is that, darling?" Bridie waited until he opened his mouth, and then popped in another spoonful of samp.

"A cave," he mumbled, his mouth full. "Not much of one, but it is a cave for all that."

Bridie nodded, and licked a dollop of sweet cornmeal from the spoon. "You shall show me your cave just as soon as you're well. Take heed!" she yelped as the bowl tipped over in her lap.

"Do you feed your poppet?" John giggled, lifting the wooden doll from the bed and wiping the cornmeal from its face.

"I see you're mending, you fresh, contrary child!" Bridie laughed, cleaning up the spill. "Now cover yourself, my lad, for I'm opening the window to let in some air. It's stuffy as an old lady's skirt in here."

John grinned at her and obediently nestled down within the covers of the bed. Bridie wished Will could see her brother now, see what a loving, sweet boy he had helped her to save. She wished she could see Will herself to thank him for that help and to thank him for keeping her secret. It was clear it had cost him dearly to take her to the heathen Indians against all the precepts of his up- bringing. But he had done so for her sake, and Bridie was filled with gratitude. She unlatched the casement and swung the window wide. As she did, she heard voices below in the street.

"Good morrow to you, Mistress MacKenzie," said Goody Furness to Bridie's mother. She was sitting across the way in the open door of her own house, carding wool.

Mistress MacKenzie shook out her broom. "And to you."

Putting aside her fleeces, the woman gave a look up and down the road, and crossed over. "People say your daughter healed your son of a strong fever," Goody Furness began.

"That she did."

"They are also saying she took her herbs and such from the savages."

Bridie stiffened. She looked down at Goody Furness's white-capped head, wishing she could be miles away, but unable to move.

"Who says she did such a thing?" Mistress MacKenzie demanded.

"The Widow Handy says it and others repeat it," replied the woman. She chose that moment to look up, and met Bridie's eyes. A hot flush swept across the woman's face, and she backed up. Bridie stared and stared, her heart drumming loud in her ears.

Mistress MacKenzie stepped out into the street and looked up at Bridie with anxious eyes. "Daughter—"

Suddenly, Bridie came out of her frozen shock and whirled around.

"Where are you going, Bridie?" John asked in surprise.

"I'll be back soon," Bridie said curtly.

With growing anger and indignation, Bridie climbed down the ladder, tore through the gathering room, and ran out the front door.

"Bridie!" her mother called as Bridie swept past.

There was no thought in Bridie's head but that Will had betrayed her and that his mother was wasting no time in spreading the news through the town. A gusty breeze pressed her clothes against her as she ran, and eyes blazing, she turned the corner to the Handys' street.

Before her was a sorry sight. The shed of the house had indeed come toppling down during the night, and the widow herself stood among the wreckage, scolding the men who were there to help her clear it away. Will also bent to the work, and the sight of him renewed Bridie's anger and outrage. Yet her heart lurched painfully as he looked up. This was not how she'd expected to meet Will again. She had looked for something finer than this treachery, and her resolve almost cracked with the pain of it. She forced him out of her mind and turned instead on his mother.

"Goody Handy!" she said, striding up to the crowd in her fury.

All stopped, startled, and turned to look at her. The Widow Handy's eyes widened, and Will shrank back against the wall of the house.

"Why do you seek to harm me, lady?" Bridie demanded. "I never wronged you."

"How do I harm her?" Goody Handy asked, turning to the others with her hands outstretched. "I stand with my house destroyed and ruined around me, and she says I seek to harm *her*?"

Bridie's eyes flashed. "You cannot say I had a hand in this destruction."

The woman reared back, her face contorted. "No? The brazen wench can say such a thing when she knows full well that she used a bent nail as a charm to do this. I have it here."

The breath left Bridie in a rush, and she clutched the fence. "What?" she gasped. There was a roaring sound in her ears. In the woman's outstretched hand lay the bent nail Bridie had so thoughtlessly picked up on the ship and so thoughtlessly tossed aside. A wild, frantic impulse to laugh rose within her and broke free. Will flushed scarlet and turned his face away.

The men standing there looked from Bridie to Goody Handy in some confusion. Goodman Devane folded his arms and frowned.

"What mischief is this?" he asked the widow. "How come you to say such a thing?"

"Do you make a charge?" Goodman Pulver demanded.

Bridie stared at Goody Handy in amazement and dread. "You do not dare to do it," she breathed, her voice shaking with anger and shock.

The widow looked around at the skeptical faces of the men, and then back at Bridie, and narrowed her eyes. "I make no *charge*," she said in a quieter tone. "But I have seen the work of witches in Salem, and this looks much like it. See how brazenly she laughs in my face. I only ask that others consider what I have seen, what has befallen me this day, what potions she sought to force on me, and what we know of her practices."

"I never practiced to do harm to anyone," Bridie replied evenly, although her head was spinning. "Though I may have cause to wish I could."

With that, she turned and stared her hard reproach at Will. He met her eyes and shook his head helplessly as the color drained from his ruddy face.

"You see how she yet conspires to bewitch my son even before our eyes!" the woman suddenly screeched and darted forward.

Bridie sprang back in alarm, pulling her skirts aside as though from the sparks of a fire. "Mistress, you wrong me," she said. "You and your son both."

She turned and walked away, feeling their wondering eyes on her back and not knowing where she went. After a few steps, she began to shiver, and tears came to her eyes. She tripped over a rock and felt the ground under her feet shift as she stepped onto the shingle of the beach. The screaming of gulls was all around, deafening her.

"How could you do it?" Bridie whispered. "How could you do it to me, Will?"

From the start, he had sought her out only in order to gather information against her. There was no other explanation that Bridie could see, and it was as though something had been ripped from her.

Now Bridie could see only the jealousy, spite, and

vindictiveness that had driven Will to her side. His friendship had been offered only as a way for his mother to hurt Bridie and her family. He'd been an instrument in his mother's hands all the time, taking home every word and gesture and deed to fuel his mother's hatred. Such a betrayal was knife and poison and hanging rope all together. Fervently Bridie wished that Will and his mother would both die.

But then she stopped herself in horror.

"Oh, Saint Bridget," she prayed. "Keep such evil thoughts from me. They'll make me what they think I am."

She stared bleakly out at the water and could not stop the tears from coming.

"Oh, God. Help me. Help me to forgive those who sin against me."

But she could not. She could not forgive them. And she would never forget. The word "witch" had been spoken aloud, and it hovered above Bridie like a carrion crow.

A roll of thunder rumbled somewhere inland, and Bridie blinked her tears away to see great clouds piling up offshore. The light began to change, yellowing and slanting as she stood crying by the water's edge.

There was a storm approaching, and Bridie could not run away from it.

Chapter Eleven

THE SQUALL ROSE swiftly on the water, turning the sky black, bucking the small boats at the moorings, and lashing rain against the windows of the houses as Bridie ran home. She was soaked before she reached Front Street, her clothes drenched and dragging. She felt as though she were drowning and soon to be pulled under. Gasping, she heaved open the door of her home.

A silent, watchful company sat in wait for her. Her parents stood together by the hearth. Several men, including the Reverend Master Stoughton, the tithing man, and one stranger, turned their eyes to look at her as she came in. With an uneasy, questioning look at her parents, Bridie shut the door behind her and leaned against it while the water from her dress puddled on the floor around her. The room was filled with the smells of wet wool, of acrid smoke, and of something smacking of the official—cold iron, black ink.

144

"What is it?" Bridie asked. Her mother came forward to wrap a cloak around her shoulders, and then went back to the fire.

"Come you in, Bridie," her father said tightly. "This man, Master Kendall, is come from the Governor General."

He indicated a tall, hawk-nosed man with hooded eyes, who sat in the best chair, his booted feet spread wide in his arrogance and authority. Kendall put his head back, staring at Bridie, taking her measure, unblinking. Here was a man who feared nothing.

"What is it?" Bridie asked again. She licked rain from her lips, suddenly thirsty. She had not been bidden to sit down. She pressed her back to the door, wishing she would not shiver from the cold, for fear they would think she was frightened.

But she was frightened. It was all she could do not to turn and claw at the door to get out.

"There have been complaints," the governor's man began. His voice was cold and dry. Bridie feared him by instinct and would have shrunk back farther but for the fact that her back was already flat to the door.

"Against me?" she whispered. "I've done no—"

"Be silent." Kendall cut her off. "Are you Catholic?"

Her eyes huge, Bridie looked at her mother. Outside, the rain continued hammering down.

"She was, sir," Mistress MacKenzie hastened to explain. "But indeed she has renounced it. She has gone to meeting these many Sabbaths since she came here."

The Reverend Stoughton shifted on the bench, fingered a button on his black coat, and then coughed into a handkerchief, squeezing his bloodshot eyes shut as he did so. Bridie looked at him vacantly, but then dragged her attention back to the governor's man.

He had taken out a paper and was holding it by its extreme edges, turning it to the light of the fire. Bridie saw a red, smoldering glow through it as he read.

"A well near Peach's Point has gone salt. Moses Marley of Beverly says the chimney of his house caught fire a fortnight ago. Hezekiah Trelawney of this town says his sow sickened and died. Fear Darton's son fell overboard and was lost at sea these three weeks since. What say you?"

Startled, Bridie looked from the paper to him. "S-sir?" she stammered. "What should I say of such mistakes and mischances?"

The men stared hard at her. "Do you deny that this is yours?" Kendall held one hand out to the tithing man, who started and reached into his coat for something. He pulled out Bridie's wooden doll and gave it to Kendall.

Bridie could feel drops of rain falling from her hair to her cheeks. All the world seemed very silent but for the rain and the crackling of flames within the hearth and Stoughton's stifled coughing.

"That is mine," she assented, not looking at her mother. "But it is only a child's toy."

"And did you place it on your brother as he lay sick even unto death?" Kendall asked.

"Yes, but it means nothing!" Bridie said. She stepped forward, hand outstretched in supplication. "Sir, it has no power to hurt nor to harm. I did nothing by giving it to my brother."

"And did not this charm aid you in your ministrations to him?" Kendall went relentlessly on. He placed the poppet on the table, where the others stole furtive glances at it.

There was a heavy pause. A log broke apart in the fire, sending a shower of sparks up the chimney.

"Am I charged?" Bridie whispered. "Am I charged with witchcraft?"

"No, no," her father spoke up. "They only question you, Daughter. Answer their questions and naught will happen."

Kendall sent Master MacKenzie a silent, hooded look, and then continued to speak, all the while staring at Bridie. "How came you to traffic with the savages, and yet they did not harm you?"

Into Bridie's mind leaped a picture of the Indians' encampment, of the laughing children and skirmishing dogs, of the women with their black, interested eyes looking at her and encouraging her in her designs. She shook her head.

"But they did not seek to harm me."

Stoughton cleared his throat. "That is what Master Kendall wishes to know. Tell us *why* did they not seek to harm you?"

Bridie spread her hands, then let them fall. "I do not know. Except why should they?"

"We have good cause to know that the savages—" Stoughton began preachingly.

"If we know they are dangerous and unaccountable," Kendall interrupted, "then we know enough. You do not deny conspiring and trafficking with them?"

Silently, Bridie shook her head.

Kendall appraised her for another moment, and then clapped his hands on his knees and stood up, drawing his damp cloak around him. Bridie's mother, unable to hold herself back any longer, rushed forward with an anguished cry.

"Sir, what charge do you make?"

Kendall's glance was so cold that Mistress MacKenzie halted.

" 'Tis not for me to make a charge," Kendall said, his voice hard and precise. "I leave that to the ones who are wronged and only investigate these reports." With a last imperious look around, he opened the door, letting in a burst of wind and rain. He left followed by the other men.

When the company were gone, Bridie began to shake, her body racked with shivering just as John's had been racked by the fever. She hugged her arms around herself. Her parents sat down heavily at the table, as though their legs had given out altogether at the end of a punishing march.

"How can such a nothing hurt us?" Master MacKenzie asked, picking up the wooden doll with a baffled frown and turning it over in his hands. He shook his head. "I'll not have it hurting us more forbye."

He made as though to throw it into the fire, but Bridie sprang forward and grabbed it from him. Her father gaped at her, looking suddenly old and confused and afraid.

"Daughter," he said.

"I'll not have my dolly destroyed." Bridie held it behind her and shook her head. "I brought so little with me from home," she added in a pleading whisper.

Her mother made a strangled sound and looked away.

"Mother!" Bridie held out one hand. "You gave this to me. And these years when I held it and cosseted it, then in my heart it was you cosseting me! Do not make me burn it for such an evil reason."

"But how—how . . ." Bridie's father trailed off, looking down into the fire. The dazed light in his eyes caused a bitter pain to Bridie and made her want to take him in her arms as she'd taken John.

"All will be well, Father," she promised, putting one hand tenderly on his arm. "You won't see it again, nor will it give anyone any trouble."

She slowly walked out of the room and climbed the ladder to where John slept. Up under the eaves, with the rain sheeting down the window and hissing on the roof, it was dark and hushed, like a cave or a twilit forest or the hold of a drifting ship. Bridie stood a moment, looking down at her sleeping brother with a feeling mixed of pain and love. His lashes cast their crescent shadows on his cheeks, the covers rose and fell with his breathing, and one hand lay curled, half open, on the pillow by his head.

"Whatever may come, I'll not regret it," Bridie whispered.

Then she turned to examine the joinery and makings of the room, where the beams came together and the posts marked the corners. Under the window, a board had been nailed to keep the drafts from seeping through, and when Bridie pulled on it, it came away, revealing a narrow gap between the sill and the studs of the wall. Narrow it was, but enough room to keep and treasure her doll.

Bridie held the small poppet against her with both hands, and through it could feel the strong beat of her own heart. It seemed almost to have a force and vitality of its own—and so it did, for it had always given her comfort and succor. Now she knew it could no longer do so for her. But it might for some other one someday.

With a tender care, Bridie laid the doll within the opening and covered it up with a cloth. Inside she also put her crucifix, taken from beside the bed. There they would be safe until some other time.

Bridie pressed the board back into place, lining up the nails with the holes. She raised her eyes to the window but could see nothing through the cold gray veil of rain.

"Can I not also hide myself away?" she whispered, her hands on the board that covered her treasures.

There was no answer to make, nor any given. God and the saints were deaf to her, or perhaps it was she who could no longer hear them.

As night fell Bridie rose from a troubled sleep. The ordinary was oddly quiet. Down the street was the sound of a dog barking and a man's voice raised in anger and the squalling of a cat suddenly cut short. The rain still came down. Shivering slightly, Bridie felt her way through the darkened room and went down the ladder.

Before she entered the gathering room, she paused, listening to her parents' voices.

"She won't be charged," Mistress MacKenzie was saying. " 'Twill all blow over like this storm."

"Charged with what?" John piped up sleepily.

"Nothing, darling. Hush."

"That may be." Master MacKenzie's voice was low and heavy. "But you see how they all stay away this night."

"I'll not serve anyone who speaks harm against my daughter, for the matter of that," Mistress MacKenzie declared.

Bridie leaned her forehead against the door frame. *Oh, Mother,* she cried silently. *What have I done?*

She pushed the door open and went in.

The place was empty but for her parents and her brother resting in their mother's arms. They turned to look at her.

Bridie gazed around her at the benches against the walls, the tankards in a row, and the blackened ceiling beams, as though for the first time.

Her mother looked swiftly to the door and then to Bridie. Her father poked at the fire.

"No one comes," John spoke up. He tipped his head back to look up at Mistress MacKenzie. "Why?"

There was a thump behind Bridie's ribs and a pricking of her fingertips. "They stay away because of me."

"No, it is only the weather keeps all men inside," Mistress MacKenzie said. "Don't fash yourself, lassie."

Bridie stood still, listening to the rain come down outside. She could almost see the streets turning to streams of mud, the houses growing black with the wet, the fires out, the boats swamped, and the sea and sky all one water. She stood still, hearing the tide rise and the rain fall, seeing the town swallowed by the sea, drowned by the sea, vanishing as though it had never been and all the people in it had melted away. She moaned.

"Bridie, lass," her father said, rising suddenly to his feet. "What is it?"

Bridie stood staring and trembling. "I fear I'll go mad," she whispered. "What if I am a witch and dinna know it? What if I've done these things they say?"

"You haven't," Mistress MacKenzie said in a sharp voice. She came to Bridie and took her by the elbows. "Look at me."

Slowly, Bridie focused her eyes on her mother's face. Mistress MacKenzie looked steadily at her, the lines about her eyes and mouth hard-etched and deep.

"You're no witch. Don't let them beat you into thinking it so, to confess what isn't true. 'Tis what happened to many of them at Salem, and that's an evil thing for certain. Deny it, for it is not true."

Bridie closed her eyes for a moment and drew in her breath. The strange mood passed from her, and she sighed, resting her head on her mother's shoulder. "What will happen to me?"

"Nothing." Mistress MacKenzie stroked Bridie's hair. "Nothing will happen to you."

She led an unresisting Bridie to the fire and pushed her gently onto a low stool. Bridie sat there, staring into the flames with the heat beating on her face: She was losing the sense of herself, stamping down her faith, checking her natural inclinations, policing every thought. Her head spun. She bent nearer, looking at the patterns that wove through the fire, feeling her skin hot and dry and tight, drawn by the beauty and power of the flames, by the pitch hissing and bubbling at the end of a burning log, by the blue heart of the fire. She reached out one hand.

"Bridie!"

She stopped and looked at her mother with a guilty start.

"Bridie, get you to bed," Mistress MacKenzie commanded.

Bridie nodded meekly, frightened and dismayed by the strangeness that kept rising up in her. She went up to bed and fell into an exhausted sleep as soon as she lay down.

Chapter Twelve

THE MORNING DAWNED blue and hot after the heavy rain. Bridie stood at the window looking out at the harbor. From her vantage point, she was apart from the town and able to see beyond it, where the freshening breeze kicked up the silvery waves. She did not want to leave the room.

"Bridie! Bridie, hurry!" came John's voice urgently from below.

Bridie pushed reluctantly away from the window and ran down to see what was the matter. John stood in the open doorway to the garden and turned fearful eyes to her.

Puzzled, Bridie brushed past him, and then was arrested by shock. Her garden was a scene of utter wreckage, the plants beaten down and the ground churned to mud. In a daze, she stepped out into it, stooping to lift the broken stems of plants and letting them fall back. She could not believe the evidence of her own eyes. "Could it ever be the rain that did this?"

With sinking heart, Bridie turned around and around, surveying the ruin of her garden. No weather could have done such a thing. Stem and leaf and twining vine were smashed to a pulp, and with each subject of destruction added one to another, Bridie felt herself closer to tears.

And then she saw her rosebush. It had been pulled wholly from the ground, and its roots lay exposed in a muddy tangle by the fence.

"Och, no!" she gasped, bending to it.

She lifted the plant tenderly, as though it were a fallen child, and pulled away the broken leaves and scraps of grass clinging to it. No rain had ruined her garden, but spite, and malice, and human hands in the darkness. Footprints were plain to see everywhere, the marks those of a small woman's shoe. Too sad to cry, Bridie pressed the rose back into the wallow of mud where it had grown. She pressed the soil around it, until she was up to her wrists in mud, pressing and pushing, silent and filled with a churning tumult of dark thoughts. Goody Handy had done this mad, violent deed. Of that she had no doubt or hesitation.

"Bridie, will it live?" John asked.

"I can't say," Bridie said through clenched teeth. One of the grafts was broken away with a ragged scar, but the other two were intact and still held their buds, swollen fat from the rain.

She stood up, wiping her muddy hands heedlessly on her apron, and gazed down the street. The day was already turning hot and steamy, and flies buzzed over the manure in the mired road. Houses on either side seemed to huddle in the muggy warmth, watching and waiting. She looked at the Furness house just in time to see Sarah pull her face back from the window. With no thought but that she must get away from those watching houses, Bridie let herself out the gate, deaf to John's voice as it followed her up Front Street.

Left up the road she went, slogging through the mud with her eyes fixed. She went past the Little Harbor, leaving the houses and climbing uphill. The hem of her skirt was heavy with mud, and although it trailed behind her at every step, she did not allow it to slow her but kilted it up impatiently with both hands. The Burial Hill was before her, and she trudged upward, only thinking to get away.

When she gained the top and was high above the town, she sat down and rested her elbows on her knees and her forehead on her folded arms. Through the crook of her elbow she looked down at the gray-green lichen that covered the rock where she sat. It grew so slowly, only inches over the many years, and yet was so hardy that sheets of ice choking and grasping it all winter long could not pry it loose. It needed little, gave little, lived long. Bridie did not think she had it in her to take any lesson from that plant. She feared she had too little toughness, too little of that nature that lay still and bided its time and endured.

As she sat with the sun warming her bared neck and the top of her head, she heard a step.

"Bridie?"

156

She went still and silent inside at the sound of Will's voice and even stopped breathing. She could not move.

"Bridie?"

"Get away from me," she whispered, and raising her voice, she repeated, "Get you away from me!"

She lifted her head to look up at him. He stood below her on the hill, holding his hat in his hands, looking lost.

"You need not follow me anymore," Bridie said icily. "You have carried information against me and have done all the damage that's required."

A wave of color swept across Will's face and ebbed away. "I never meant to harm you. That I swear."

"That you swear?" Bridie stood up awkwardly in her muddied clothes and staggered to one side as her skirt tripped her. She glared as he made a move to aid her.

"That you swear, Will Handy?" she repeated. "And do you swear you never thought it would do me harm to tell folk I was a witch? Nor thought it would harm me to tell folk I conspired with the savages or sought to bewitch you when it was always, *always* you that came after me?"

He could only shake his head mutely, and Bridie wanted to hit him, slap his face, beat him with a stick, anything to make him cry out in heat and passion. But she felt sick and turned away. From the corner of her vision, she saw the crab tree and felt bitter tears fill her throat.

"I rue it, I do," Will said. "My mother bade me tell her of you, and I must obey her."

"And I'll swear she does not rue anything," Bridie

muttered, sitting down again as the heat and strength flooded out of her.

Will knelt beside her, and it pained her to see the blue of his eyes. "I begged her not repeat it, but she was adamant as she has never been before."

Bridie looked away at the water and the clouds that raced over the ocean. Her heart continued to beat inside her, although she could not think how it could. "Do you think I am a witch?" she asked quietly.

The clouds scudded onward like ships, the wind soughed in the tops of the trees below them, and a gull winged slowly across Bridie's vision and plunged down toward the water and out of sight. Will made no answer.

Bridie turned to look at him, to memorize the planes and curves of his handsome face. He dropped his gaze before her steady scrutiny.

"And so you do think I am a witch," Bridie said. "And would you dare God and risk damnation for me?"

He still made no answer, but took one of her hands and rubbed his thumb gently over a dried clot of mud, looking at it. Bridie thought her heart must break.

"I could have loved you," she whispered.

Before he could answer her, she pulled her hand away and struggled to her feet, and hurried down the hill. But she could not go into the town. She turned toward Salem and made for the point of land called Peach's, which jutted out into the ocean like a fist.

When at last she was at the end, she stood on the rocky promontory with the wind whipping her hair around her face so that it stung her cheeks and eyes. She stared east, where the clouds made green shadows speed over the water and the sturdy ships made for Scotland.

She could not go back. There was nothing there, nothing in Arrochar. She could never stand under Ben Lomond and hear the eagles screaming high above, nor see the sky at night gleam red and green and white with the aurora. That had always seemed like a heavenly host to her, looking down with saintly protection. There were no saints looking down on Massachusetts and no way to get back to where they were.

Few came that day to the MacKenzie ordinary, and on the next morning, there was a stain and stench of rotten egg on the door. Bridie felt the sting and slap of her outcastness each time she stepped into the street, keeping her eyes down and her head bowed. She saw the Reverend Stoughton in conversation with some women who stared at her and then pointedly turned their backs.

For herself Bridie did not really care, but her family was suffering, and Bridie knew no remedies, no cures, no medicines to take away the malady that gripped them all together. She was the disease.

Three days had gone by since Kendall's ominous visit, and Bridie made for the harbor, looking to buy some fish. Up ahead stood Mistress Carter with little Margaret by the hand. Bridie felt a surge of relief when she saw them, knowing that they at least would not consider her wicked simply for her faith.

"Good day to you," she said as she came up behind them.

Mistress Carter turned, and her eyes widened when she saw Bridie. Margaret smiled and made to run forward, but her mother pulled the little girl closer to her, which brought the blackness flooding into Bridie's heart again.

"Mama, what is it?" the child asked. " 'Tis Bridie."

"Be silent, Margaret," Mistress Carter scolded. "We cannot tarry."

Bridie shook her head with melancholy regret. "Had I not used my medicines for your daughter, there would have been ample for John," she whispered. "I'd have had no cause to seek the Indians' help." She swallowed the sourness in her mouth as she looked at Mistress Carter.

"I can't help that. What's done is done."

"You shun me too?" Bridie asked.

The woman's face colored, and she looked nervously around to see who watched them. Several women walked by, and though they did not stare, their steps slowed and they appeared to listen. "They say—"

"But what say you?" Bridie cut in. She reached for Mistress Carter's hand and clutched it for a moment before it was pulled away. "It is because I am Catholic, and because I can heal. Surely you of all people have good reason not to hate these things in me."

Bridie looked down at Margaret. The child smiled at her uncertainly. "Will you come—" she began, but Mistress Carter pushed her daughter behind her.

"We have no protection to offer to you now," Mistress Carter whispered, still looking anxiously to and fro. "I

160

cannot let them think I support you, or they'll turn their questions toward me. Now let me by."

Bridie stood aside, watching dully as her former friend hurried away. In a rush and confusion of thoughts, Bridie saw that this was how a person might become as Goody Handy was, filled with malice toward all, clutching at the shreds of love with grasping claws even as it fled. Bridie was filled with sick loathing and dread. She could not let herself become as Will's mother was.

But she did not see how to avoid it if her portion continued to be so bitter.

Help me bear it, she prayed fervently. Help me bear it and keep me from despair. Let me not give in, for then I am surely damned.

She left the harbor, and when she returned to the house without fish, her mother said nothing. For the rest of the day, Bridie sat by the fire in the empty gathering room, shivering in spite of the heat and letting her thoughts wander among misery, faint hope, and angry protestation. Mistress MacKenzie placed a bowl of fish stew by her side, and Bridie knew it was evening, but she did not move.

By night, her limbs were stiff and tired, and she wondered vaguely if they might crack and she might crumble into dust. She almost hoped she would, for then there'd be nothing left but ashes when Kendall returned, as return he was bound to do if a single slight misfortune harmed anyone in town. And in such a place, misfortunes rushed in with every tide. The next crippled foal, the next leaking boat, the next slip and fall would be blamed on her.

"Bridie, lass." Master MacKenzie's step sounded on the floor beside her. He placed one hand on her shoulder. "This will all pass over, for folk have greater cares to trouble them. Hearten yourself."

Bridie rested her head back against him, her eyes lingering on the hypnotic fire. "Why did you not bring me with you when you came?" she murmured, ignoring his advice.

"We thought it best. God knows that we did."

"What will I do?" Bridie whispered half to herself.

Her father pulled her to her feet and shook her none too gently. "We canna go back! Go forward, Bridie, and leave off this melancholy humor of yours. It will kill you. You mun go forward."

Chastened, Bridie nodded. "I will, Father. I will try."

She roused herself and looked around. Where the room should have been loud and full of men, there were only empty benches. Her family would be destitute if nothing changed to stave it off. Bridie walked slowly to the door and went out, looking for an answer.

In the darkness, she wandered down the street. She knew she did herself no good by it, for folk would think her strange if they saw her. But only out near the water was the air clear enough to blow away the cobwebs that kept wreathing around her and clouding her eyes. Already she felt better and stronger. She berated herself for slipping into such a morbid frame of mind, for that meant she was giving up.

Her steps grew longer and her back straighter as she walked. She could hear the gentle sighing of waves on the shingle, of water pooling around the rocks as the tide rose. Even the town itself was less watchful at night, as the darkness made one thing out of many. Bridie walked along a crooked street, gathering her thoughts and her courage.

Then, just up ahead, she heard the uneasy, peevish squealing of pigs. She quickened her steps and saw a figure melting into the shadows near the Carters' house with slow stealth. In the air was a faint, acrid tang, as though someone had passed with a shuttered lantern. Bridie stopped, straining to see ahead in the dark, and waited.

And then a flicker of light leaped out of the black night, and in a moment, flames began creeping up the side of the building. Bridie's heart jolted within her.

"Fire!" Bridie shouted, turning to throw her voice in all directions. "Fire!"

She ran forward to rouse the Carters from their beds, and saw the same furtive shadow racing away. Without thinking, she leaped ahead and made a wild grab at the air where the running figure was, and her fingers closed around the rough woolen cloth of a full-skirted dress.

"Let loose!" the woman screamed demonically, beginning to struggle and fight. "Let loose!"

Bridie nearly let go in her shock. Doors banged open, windows were thrown wide, torches and lanterns lit, and voices roused to action. In the street, people were beginning to run toward the Carter house, shouting out instructions and alarms. Bridie dragged her captive toward the crowd, trying to get to some light. With a gasp, she yanked the woman forward and saw that it was Goody Handy.

"What goes on here?" cried out Master Bowman when he saw them.

"It was she who made the fire!" Goody Handy screeched, her eyes glittering in the light of the flames. "I saw her with my own eyes!"

Bridie sucked in her breath. The air was filled with smoke and with the great confusion of yells and barking dogs and folk passing buckets of water from the beach to the house.

"It was not I who did it," Bridie said, throwing back her head. "I was passing and saw Goody Handy."

Her face contorted with rage, the widow began to denounce Bridie in a high-pitched voice. "I saw the witches at Salem, I know their tricks and devices! Heed me! She's wicked! Don't listen to anything she says or you, too, will be bewitched."

Bowman stepped back in dismay, and others gathered around, faces blackened with soot and gleaming damply in the hellish light.

"It's that artful girl," an angry voice said.

"They say she's a witch," another said in rising panic.

"She is a witch!" screamed Goody Handy, her eyes glistening with hatred. "She has done this!"

Bowman tried to calm the ranting woman, but she would not be held or quietened. Bridie stood trembling, knowing that none could witness such a frenzy without knowing the woman was mad.

Mistress Carter stumbled toward her. "What have you done to us?" she wailed at Bridie.

"What did we do that you should hurt us?" Master Carter asked dazedly.

Stunned, Bridie held out her hands, but Mistress Carter only shrank back and began to sob. Margaret clung to her mother's skirt, crying in fear and bewilderment.

"You see? You all see!" shrieked Goody Handy. "She's evil! Burn her! That's fitting judgment!"

"Stay, stay!" Bowman roared as the crowd surged forward in hysterical confusion. Goody Handy continued to scream invectives, rousing the people even more, while Trelawney darted among the firelit crowd like a fiend, speaking into ears and pointing at Bridie.

"My sow that died," Trelawney said. "I've good reason to think *she* done it. And there's more I could tell!"

"Mother!" Will ran up to the mob and took her arm. "Mistress MacKenzie—what is this?"

Bridie backed away from him. She felt potent fear, but also disgust and amazement. "It was her design all along to discredit me and my family, and to punish me for caring for her son. Now she has overstepped reason and started a fire, hoping it will burn me, too, in the end."

"No," Will said, shaking his head.

"We don't know who started the fire," Goodman Devane spoke up. "It may have been mischance."

Bridie stared at Will. "You know she has compelled you to give information against me. Do not deny it!" She would not let him look away from her until he answered.

"She's a liar!" Goody Handy spat. She threw her arms

wide. "See how calmly she stands there, an affront to God and man, and twists the truth around."

"Lady, lady," Master Bull said gruffly. "Take care of what slanders you make."

The fire was out, and the men and women who had been fighting it now swelled the ranks of the crowd standing around. Folk murmured among themselves. Sarah Furness and her parents were there, staring mutely about but not looking at Bridie.

"Some of you know I am not what this woman says," Bridie called out. "Will you not speak for me?"

Sarah met Bridie's eyes and opened her mouth to speak. But even as hope rose in Bridie's heart, Sarah looked away without a word and backed into the crowd. Bridie could not feel sad. Other losses loomed too large.

She turned to Will. "You know your mother has conspired to hurt me because she fears that you care for me. Tell these people that it's true, for you know it is."

Will looked at her, pain and grief evident in his face. "I do—"

"No!" Goody Handy ran forward, hands reaching for Bridie's face. Several men leaped to restrain her, and Bridie fell back. Will stared at his mother with an expression of pain and disbelief pulling his features awry. He looked as though he might cry.

"Make way—let us by!"

Bridie's parents shouldered through the crowd to Bridie's side just as a clod of mud sailed through the air and landed at her feet. Mistress MacKenzie put her arms around her daughter.

"You know us to be good and God-fearing people," Master MacKenzie said loudly. "Why do you turn against us only on this woman's word?" Bridie trembled within her mother's arms, fighting not to tumble into darkness.

"Bridget MacKenzie has no cause or reason to kindle a fire here," Master Penworthy suggested to the crowd. "Yet if what the girl says is true, I can see reason enough for Goody Handy."

Mutters of agreement ran through the crowd. Bowman rubbed his chin and shook his head. "These are matters to discuss in daylight," he said in his rumbling bass.

"Aye, for darkness gives comfort to some," came a voice from the crowd. "It was not the widow who did those other things. Calling on saints—consorting with savages."

Bridie looked around her. "Yet it was she who painted them with such a black brush. I have no witchcraft in me and never harmed any person here or anywhere." She turned to the Carters for support one last time, wishing they would remember their debt to her but still unwilling to tell the crowd of their faith.

"Liar," Will's mother said. Tears ran unheeded down her face. "You should be hanged. You're wicked!"

"No, Mother," Will said brokenly. "No one will be hanged. Come home, now."

Without another word, Will took his mother's arm and led her away. Still she was shouting. "You'll rue this! You'll soon see what harm she may do!"

"Quiet the woman," someone counseled. "The MacKenzies may bring a charge of slander against her."

"Not if it's the truth."

"You're proving yourself an idiot—"

"As are you."

As the words darted around her, Bridie stood still where she was, shielded by her parents but not protected by them. She knew that even now, Will would not abandon his mother, malevolent and mad though she was. Bridie straightened and stepped out of her mother's embrace.

"I tell you now," she said to Master Bowman and Master Bull and Goodman Devane and the other men. "You wrong me and my family if you do not see that this woman has twisted my words and actions since I arrived. And you do yourself wrong if you allow yourself to fear such wicked gossip."

"Aye, I hear you well," Bowman agreed slowly.

"The widow does seem mad ofttimes," Devane added.

At once Bridie felt the last shreds of strength run out of her, and she felt her knees begin to shake. She turned and walked away, her parents taking her arms, and the crowd parted silently as they went. Murmurs of encouragement followed her as she left, but still some people pulled away from her and watched her cautiously.

"Hush, now," Mistress MacKenzie murmured to Bridie, her own voice shaking with fear. "Hush. We have you."

Bridie stood at the window in the morning, looking at the harbor, refusing to squint against the harsh, bright reflected light. She would not let herself be bowed down by the brisk, brash forward urge of Massachusetts any longer. She would not submit to it, would not let it break her and mold her into a shadow of herself. But that meant she had to walk away from it. And so she stood at her lookout, shading her eyes to see the leap and toss of waves and the foaming rush of the currents that drove past her, wondering when she would ever make landfall.

From the corner of her eyes, she could see someone walking up the street, stopping below and gazing up at her. But she was too absorbed in the brittle beauty of the light and the streaming strength of the ocean to look down. This was one thing she would sorely miss, this view, and she drank it in hungrily.

"Bridie."

With an effort, she dragged her eyes away and looked below. Will stood in the road before her house with his head tipped back and the sun on his shoulders. Bridie leaned out the window, shaking her head. She felt as though she were speeding backward furiously fast and almost reached out one hand so he could keep her from washing away. But she did not reach out, and she did not speak. With a baffled look, he turned and walked away.

Bridie collected the bundle of clothes that she'd tied in her cloak. At the door of the room, she looked back to the place where her doll and her cross were hidden. There they would stay, buried testaments.

When she had climbed down the ladder, she went

out and stood in the garden. It still bore the traces of Goody Handy's destruction, but even so, the plants were struggling to restore themselves. Bridie bent to pull some sprouted weeds, easing her heart for a moment with the smell of the earth. She felt the solid comfort of the ordinary behind her. Turning, she reached out to touch the building, and the weathered gray shingles were warm beneath her hand.

The door opened, and Mistress MacKenzie stepped out into the fresh light. She looked anxiously at Bridie. "How are you, darling, after last night?"

"As you would expect," Bridie replied, sitting back on her heels and wiping her brow. "As you would expect."

Her mother came close and put one hand on Bridie's shoulder. "There, now, don't let it—" She broke off abruptly. "What is this?"

Bridie followed her mother's gaze to the bundle of clothes that lay to the side of the door, mute but full of meaning. Bridie's heart pounded dully at the thought of what she must do.

"What does this mean?" Mistress MacKenzie asked with alarm.

"I'm going to New France," Bridie said unsteadily. She couldn't look at her mother but kept her eyes on the spiky gray stems of a lavender plant.

"Daughter, Daughter." Her mother knelt beside Bridie and put her arms around her. "Don't do this. You mustn't leave. This is wrong."

Bridie closed her eyes. She was trembling. "I heard there is a ship at Salem that is sailing north, and I can make passage to Quebec." Her voice cracked, but she went on. "I can't stay here. If I'd come with you long ago, it would have been different. But I can't learn to be what I am not."

"No, you mustn't say such things. 'Tis only the fear and the shock of last night that makes you want to flee. 'Twill all pass."

"No, Mother." Bridie buried her face in her mother's breast. "It won't."

"What's this?" came Master MacKenzie's hearty voice. "What do you both in the dirt, there?"

"Ian—" Mistress MacKenzie rose to her feet, pulling Bridie up with her. "Ian—"

Bridie's father took in their tears and Bridie's baggage. He began to shake his head.

"What is it?" John asked, joining his father at the door.

"I'm leaving, Johnny," Bridie said. "I cannot bide here anymore."

"What do you mean?" John asked, his eyes widening. "Why can't you bide with us?"

"Because I can't, my bonny boy," Bridie said. She blinked hard. "I don't belong here and would always be an outsider."

She looked at her parents, whose faces were drawn with guilt and dismay, and though she feared she was crushing them, she forced herself to go on. "Last night— 'twas only the beginning, for folk will always harbor a suspicion of me."

"No, my girl. You need not go." Master MacKenzie

strode forward and took her by the arms. "Your place is with us. Do not let them say they drove a witch away. If you go, they will believe they were right to suspect you and will warn others against us."

Bridie hung her head. "There is no way to put it right, no matter what I do," she said bitterly.

"Then stay, Bridget," Master MacKenzie insisted. "And you will prove them wrong. These rumors and gossips will turn elsewhere, and we can weather it."

"No, I know it—it cannot be," Bridget said. "The people may know I am no witch, yet I am not one of them. I am not part of this place."

Her mother took Bridie's hand and held it as though she would never release it. "You must not—I cannot lose another child."

Bridie's heart was cracking. "I've saved Johnny for you. You have him. But if I stay here, you'll lose everything. I cannot change. And someone will hurt you for that."

"Oh, my girl." Mistress MacKenzie sighed. "We never looked for this."

Master MacKenzie opened his mouth to speak but could not. He looked suddenly old, and Bridie was cut deep by the sight of tears on his cheeks. She who'd never wished to do anything but join her family must now leave them and kill their dreams. Behind them all rose the bulk of the ordinary, gray as a headstone. It would never be her home now, though it sheltered everything she loved. She was exiled from its heart and hearth.

"This is hard, hard," she whispered, putting one

hand over her eyes and seeing again the bleak bare hills of Scotland blown by a northern wind.

John tugged at Bridie's sleeve. "Why? Tell me why?"

Crying, Bridie bent down and looked him in the face and ran one finger tenderly across the freckles on his nose. "I fear I can't tell you anything you'll understand. I must go, but dinna forget me."

She stood up and turned away so that she did not have to look at his bright eyes and well-loved face. "You'll have to have the charge of my garden now, John. Remember all I've told you. Let us see how my roses do," Bridie said with a brightness she thought she'd never truly feel again.

She went to the sunny corner where the fence met the house, and stopped short. Before her, the rosebush had unfurled its blooms, answering the call of summer despite its uprooting. The blossoms blazed crimson against the green leaves, and a bee hovered in drunken delight above the glorious flowers.

"Look," Bridie whispered. She touched the silky petals with one finger, and almost heard her grandfather's voice in her ear. Her heart was so full she thought it would burst. "See how it thrives here."

Mistress MacKenzie put her arms around Bridie and held her close. "My darling daughter," she said. "I wish you could too."

For a moment, Bridie let herself believe she could, and rested her cheek against her mother's shoulder. Then she pushed away, wiping her eye. "No, I'd live, but I fear I'd be a sorry, stunted thing."

Her father cleared his throat gruffly. "It is a bonny red rose, Bridie. It'll be the envy of all who pass here."

"Then call this place the Rose," Bridie suggested. "Like the boat that carried me here." She bent over the plant and carefully broke away one stem. "It may be I can graft it again in another place."

Her mother's face went as white as a ship's sail, and she clenched her fists by her sides. "Bridget," she said as tears spilled unheeded down her face.

Bridie hugged her parents each in turn and kissed them. Then she held her brother tightly to her before putting him roughly aside. "Good-bye. I'll find someone to write a letter to you."

"No, Bridie—" John cried out, but his mother caught him and folded him into her arms. The boy sobbed and kicked against her, but Mistress MacKenzie was as rigid as stone.

Bridie's father dug in his pocket and put all his shillings and crowns into Bridie's hand. "You cannot leave penniless," he said in a choked voice. "You mun have aught to sustain you."

Bridie looked down at the silver and gold glittering in her palm. "I do not know where I go or what I'll find there, but I have weathered much before this, and I can survive the next."

She tilted her hand, and the coins flashed brilliantly into her eyes, as though she held the sun and stars in her grasp. She'd been orphaned before, and something in her had grown strong. Bridie was being orphaned again, but by her own choice, and that meant that she had more than money to sustain her.

"After some time . . ." Master MacKenzie said hoarsely. "After some time you might return to us."

Bridie looked at her father. She had waited ten years for the chance to return to them. And she feared now it would never come again. But she nodded. "I pray so."

Then she stepped away quickly for fear of losing her courage. She could hardly see through her tears. Fumbling with the gate, she went into the street. Will, sitting on the front step of the Furness house, rose to his feet, and Bridie turned to him in surprise.

"I want to do something for you," Will said. "Anything that will help you."

Bridie felt dizzy with disappointment and sorrow. "Take me to the Salem ferry," she said.

"What?" He shook his head, looking past her at her family.

"Convey me there," Bridie pleaded, praying she would not break down. "Do."

Reluctantly Will took her bundle, and Bridie walked beside him up Front Street. They did not speak as they went, for Bridie was too full of grief at losing her family, nor did she know yet what she could say to him. She did not look at him. For all he had done and failed to do, she still felt the tie between them that she could not understand. It grieved her sorely that she could not hate him. She feared she loved him. Nor could she leave without finding out how much he cared for her.

As they crested the hill, the ferry landing came into sight below them. Across the wide expanse of water that separated Marblehead from Salem, Bridie could just make out the edge of land. Will stopped her, and they stood in the full force of the ocean wind, which forced tears into their eyes. At the landing, the boatman was splicing a rope, heedless of the anguished couple above him.

"Say something," Bridie whispered. " 'Tis still not too late for you to *say* something to me!"

"I would this were otherwise," Will said, looking down into her eyes. "I can't say why my mother hates you so, but know that I've tried to change her. I fear she has lost her reason."

Nodding, Bridie started forward again down the slope to the water. It was so bitter to hear him acknowledge it at this late hour when it came too late to sustain her. She did not know how she would make it to the boat without flying into pieces.

Then she stumbled and felt Will's arms catch her and hold her tight. She clung to him suddenly, fiercely, unable to believe that she was leaving him behind. She pressed her face to the rough wool of his Puritan coat. "Come with me."

His cheek rested against her hair. "Bridie." It was a sigh.

"We can make a new start in New France," she whispered. She could feel him tremble. "Come with me."

"If I—"

"Go you to Salem?" the ferryman called up.

Bridie did not answer. Will released her.

"Is it true a ship sails north to New France?" Will asked hoarsely.

"Aye, the Dutch ship *Hope* of Rotterdam leaves Salem this day." The man spat over the side of the dock into the water. "Do you take passage on her?"

Bridie clenched her fists at her side. Gulls keened overhead, their cries whipped away by the wind. "Do you?" she whispered, her eyes on Will's face.

Then, behind him, she saw a dark figure appear at the top of the hill, and her face fell in dismay.

Will turned, following her gaze, and stiffened. Goody Handy's hair was wild, her dress flapping around her in the wind, and her eyes were wide and vacant. "Will?" she croaked. "Don't leave me!"

"Oh, Mother." Will's voice was taut with pain.

Tears sprang to Bridie's eyes. She knew what his decision must be, where his duty and obedience—and burden —lay. Taking her belongings, she climbed down into the boat and took a seat in the stern with her back to the land. But the ferryman hefted the oars, sculling the boat about until it pointed away from Marblehead, and Bridie faced Will once again. She could not help but watch him as the small craft plunged into the waves. The wind helped them out, and Bridie was shocked to see how quickly the shore fell away.

Will stood on the rocks as upright as ever he had been. But he raised one hand.

"God go with you," he shouted over the breeze.

Bridie nodded. "And with you," she whispered. "Dinna forget me, Will of God Handy."

Then she turned to look out over the water where they headed, away from Marblehead, and toward a new home.

Meet the next generation of the MacKenzie family in Wild Rose Inn #2: *Ann of the Wild Rose Inn*, coming soon.

Marblehead, Massachusetts—1774

On the eve of the Revolutionary War, Ann MacKenzie must choose between her duty to a fledgling nation and her love for an enemy soldier.

Roger sighed contentedly and looked out at the surf. "Ah, it's good to have summer. Do you know that song, 'The Winter It Is Past'?"

Ann blushed and backed away out of the water. "I may become a philosopher, but never a singer, I fear."

"Come, I'll never believe it," Roger said with a grin. "Only follow me."

"I can't, I say," Ann protested, laughing anyway.

" 'Oh, the winter it is past, and the summer's come at last—' " Roger sang in a fine, husky baritone that Ann heard in her heart. " 'And the small birds sing in every tree.' "

Ann put both hands over her mouth and shook her head.

"Come, follow it," Roger persisted. " 'Oh, the winter it is past—' "

Ann shook her head in resignation, and the breeze flirted with a strand of her hair, tossing it across her eyes. "I've given you fair warning . . ." Drawing a deep breath, she repeated the line in such an off key that Roger winced.

"You're playing," he said.

"I play not." Ann laughed, pulling the hair away from her face. "I did say I could not sing a note. I have no tricks in me."

"No," he said, his eyes lingering on her face. "I see that now."

Ann swallowed with some difficulty. She could not hide that she liked him. "Do you stay here long in Marblehead port?" she asked shyly.

"Perhaps." He turned abruptly away, a frown pulling his mouth down, and began to walk back to the rocks.

Puzzled and hurt, Ann watched him, her heart pounding. The lightness had suddenly gone from the day, and she felt the sting of humiliation.

Roger stopped and turned back to her. Ann's hopes rose instantly. "If you see me in the town, you may choose not to know me," he said unaccountably.

"What? I don't understand."

Roger bent over, reaching behind a boulder, and then stood up. Ann's gaze dropped to his hand—in which he held a uniform jacket of the British navy. The enemy! The sand suddenly seemed to give way beneath Ann's feet, and she stared at him through tears of betrayal.

Then she scooped up her shoes and ran, stumbling, back toward the town.

Read the intriguing saga of
Ann of the Wild Rose Inn.

ABOUT THE AUTHOR

Jennifer Armstrong is the author of many books for children and young adults, including the historical novel *Steal Away*, the Pets, Inc. series, and several picture books.

Ms. Armstrong lives in Saratoga Springs, New York, in a house more than 150 years old that is reputed to have been a tavern. In addition to writing, Ms. Armstrong raises guide-dog puppies and works in her garden, where roses grow around the garden gate.

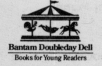

STARFIRE

Outstanding Fiction for Today's Teen!

A FAMILY APART, ORPHAN TRAIN QUARTET, BOOK 1 by Joan Lowery Nixon

☐ 27478-3 $3.99

Here is the first in an exciting 4-part historical series. The first book is the story of six children whose poverty-stricken mother makes the ultimate sacrifice of love—she sends them west on the Orphan Train to find better lives. Frances Mary, the eldest, tells of her family's adventures on their journey and after they settle into their new lives.

> "This exciting and touching novel projects an aura of historical reality." —*School Library Journal*

Look for

☐ 27912-2   **CAUGHT IN THE ACT,**
              ORPHAN TRAIN QUARTET, BOOK 2 $3.50

☐ 28196-8   **IN THE FACE OF DANGER, BOOK 3** $3.99

☐ 28485-1   **A PLACE TO BELONG, BOOK 4** $3.50